No I

GW00789365

The magical a~~~ mysterious

Madame Mistral

Herbert's story

"What is your favourite animal?"

(You'll know why when you read the book!)

Paul Delaney

[signature]

Saturday 20ᵗʰ June 2020.

First published in 2015 by FeedARead.com

Text © Paul Richard Delaney

Illustrations © Danny Long

Design © The Pig tourist publishing

A CIP catalogue record for this title is available from the British Library

www.pdelaney.co.uk

Paul Delaney is a poet, a writer and a professional organist. He's also a dad to three brilliant, super sporty and trendy boys, called Harry, George and Freddie.

Paul enjoys lots of things, including caravanning, walking and burning things in the kitchen. His favourite culinary creation is beans on toast with grated cheddar cheese on the top! And a tomato, obviously. Then again, he has just discovered a slow cooker…

This is Paul's fourth book for children:

Others include:
(All available in paperback / kindle)

Sparrowlegs

I'm fed up! (poetry)

My toilet is a murderer!

This book is dedicated to

**Grace, Lewie and Zara
and families**

For when one parent suddenly
flies up to heaven,

life changes

but a strange,
inner strength
is found…

Because love
never dies...

ONE

CRASH. Herbert's fingers slipped through the climbing frame's bars. BANG. His knees thumped into the cold, solid metal. WOLLOP. His body dropped through the air, plunging into the crash-mats below. Stars spun around Herbert's head.

'How many fingers am I holding up?' Mr Skelhorn asked.

'Err, three,' Herbert groaned.

'That's right,' Mr Skelhorn replied, looking into Herbert's eyes.

'Sorry, Sir,' Herbert said. 'I've been afraid of heights ever since I fell out of my pram when I was a baby.'

'Oh come on, Herbert,' Mr Skelhorn chuckled, shaking his head. 'You're not exactly climbing up Blackpool tower, are you?'

The children in Herbert's group launched laughter bombs.

'Come on Herb,' Joe shouted, pointing at the climbing frame. 'Anybody can climb to the top of that thing!'

'It's great if you're Spiderman,' Herbert shouted back, rubbing his knees.

'You'll have to face your fear of heights, Herbert,' Mr Skelhorn whispered into his pupil's ear. 'You never know what's around the corner!'

'Well I'm not exactly planning on scaling the Empire State building just yet, Sir,' Herbert remarked, jumping to his feet. 'I'll leave that one to King Kong thanks!'

'Try taking the elevator,' Skelhorn chuckled. 'It's a lot easier.'

The school bell sounded. Another school day ended. Marching across the playground, Herbert and his best friends Joe and Jack, giggled together.

'You've got to laugh though, Herb,' Joe said, kicking a football across the tarmac. 'A kid from the nursery could probably climb higher than you.'

'Funny!' Herbert replied, spreading his lips into a smile. 'I'll show you all one day, when I'm at the top of Mount Everest, especially Skelhorn!'

'Yeah, in your dreams, Herb,' Jack said.

Herbert pushed his hand through his thick, brown hair. He stopped, looking towards the school gates. 'Oh no, looks like that Trevor's picking me up again,' he said, puffing out a long blow.

'Who's he?' Joe asked, his green eyes sinking into his face.

'Mum's new boyfriend,' Herbert replied, dragging his bag across the playground. 'She's only been with him for a few weeks and he's already staying most weekends.'

'Looks ok to me,' Jack said.

'Yeah but look at him,' Herbert snapped. 'He's a gorilla! His jeans and t-shirt are about three sizes too small and he's covered in that spray tan stuff. How sad's that?'

'Well he's only trying his best,' Joe said. 'I walk home on my own every day, Herb. I'd love it if my dad picked me up but he's always in work.'

'My dad picked me up once,' Jack chuckled, flashing his teeth. 'When I fell over ice skating!'

Laughter rang out as Joe and Jack sprinted away. 'See you on Monday, Herb!' they both shouted, throwing their backpacks over their shoulders.

TWO

'Good day today, mate?' Trevor asked, ruffling up Herbert's hair with a big, fat hand. Herbert moved away, dragging his feet on the pavement. 'Not bad,' he snapped, looking the other way. 'And by the way, I'm not your mate!'

'Do anything interesting?' Trevor asked, ignoring Herbert's razor sharp reply.

'No!'

'Nothing at all?'

'No!'

'Come on, you must have done something.'

'I did nothing!' Herbert barked, his jaws snapping up and down. 'I've told you, haven't I?'

'All right,' Trevor said, shaking his head. 'Keep your hair on.'

Hardly a word was spoken all the way home. 'Fancy a bar of chocolate?' Trevor asked as they passed the corner shop. 'No thanks,' Herbert replied, increasing his pace.

'What about a play around in the park then?'

'No thanks; I've got tonnes of homework to do! And anyway, we don't have a ball, so what's the point?'

'I can easily whizz home and get the rugby ball,' Trevor said. 'Or the football.'

'I've told you Trevor, I don't want to play anything,' Herbert said, his voice rising into a half shout. 'So just leave me alone.'

Puffing out a long, loud breath of air, Trevor pushed his hands deep into his jeans' pockets. 'Ok I get the picture. Calm down mate!'

'I'm not your mate, Trevor!' Herbert bawled, his words as sharp as porcupine spines. 'And I never will be, so just leave me alone.'

Those words plunged into Trevor's chest, deflating his mood.

Trevor cast his eyes over the little, jagged cracks in the pavement. *You can only try your best,* he thought, his mind clouded by a hazy mist.

Herbert increased his pace, trotting away. Trevor followed, several steps behind. He glanced up at Herbert, asking him to slow down. But Herbert took no notice.

After a cold, silent walk home, Herbert bounced on the top of his bed. Holding his iPad above his face, he clicked onto a game and buried his thoughts.

'Fancy a drink, Herbert?' Trevor shouted, his voice drifting up the stairs.

'No thanks!' Herbert replied. *And do me a favour will you?* he thought. *Go and get lost!*

'Are you sure?' Trevor asked. 'Mum's bought that strawberry smoothie you like.'

'No I'm fine, thanks,' Herbert replied. 'I'm not thirsty!'

And I'll be even finer if you stay where you are, he thought.

Trevor climbed the stairs. 'Room for another player?' he asked, appearing at Herbert's bedroom door. 'Yes, but I've just finished,' Herbert said, not pulling his eyes away from his game's colourful graphics.

Leaning over, Trevor grabbed Herbert's iPad and switched it off. 'What on earth do you think you're doing?' Herbert yelled. 'You're not my dad!'

'I'll never be your dad, Herbert,' Trevor said, raising his blonde eyebrows. 'And to be honest, I'm not trying to be.'

'Well it certainly feels like it to me,' Herbert replied, punching his duvet with two hard, clenched fists. Trevor stared into Herbert's face, his big eyes widening. 'Just remember, eh?' he said. 'This is hard for me too.'

Herbert's mum pushed open the front door. 'Hi everybody!' she shouted. 'I'm home!'

Springing off his bed, Herbert rushed downstairs. Throwing his arms around her, he squeezed into his mum's blouse, hugging her warm body. 'Where've you been, Mum?'

'Oh you know what school's like,' his mum replied, rubbing her son's back. 'Sometimes, you just can't get away! Anyway, was Trevor waiting for you?'

'Yes he was,' Herbert answered, screwing up his face. 'And he was embarrassing me as usual, in front of all my mates!'

'Oh don't start all that again,' Mum said, looking into a mirror.

She peered at her reflection. Moving closer, she touched her face with her long, manicured nails. A pleasing image looked out at her. She stared into her bright blue eyes, massaging the delicate skin under them.

She had a striking, oval face and a full head of long, blonde hair. A thin film of flesh coloured make-up and a layer of bright red lipstick completed the picture.

'If you had your way, Herbert,' she said, 'I'd be on my own for the rest of my life.'

'I know but Dad…'

'Dad died five years ago,' Mum said. 'And I know it's really hard, Herbert, but, well, we just have to try to get on with it.'

'I know but we've not been to Dad's grave for weeks now,' Herbert said, folding his arms tight. 'Well I've been busy with school and anyway, Dad always said it's best to have his picture around the house. And the place is full of them!'

'Can we go tomorrow?' Herbert asked.

'We'll go to the cemetery at the weekend; Promise you,' Mum said, stroking her son's face. 'How about Sunday afternoon?'

'Well as long as that Trevor doesn't come,' Herbert said. 'I mean Dad would hate it if he turned up – he's boring and he thinks he's cool and - '

'Hey now, don't say that,' Mum snapped, interrupting her son's flow. 'Trevor's alright you know, you just have to get used to him.'

'Yes but it's like getting used to a hole in your head,' Herbert said, following his mum into the warm, spacious lounge. 'And I still miss Dad!'

Tears spilled out of Herbert's eyes. 'Hey now, stop it,' his mum said, wrapping her long arms around him. Squeezing into his body, she soothed Herbert's sadness like a guardian angel.

'And I miss him too, love,' Mum said, her own tears welling up in those bright, blue eyes of hers. 'And I think of him every single day,' she added, her quivering voice fragile and faint.

'I see his face and hear his laugh. I can even smell his aftershave sometimes but it's only in my dreams, because Rob's in heaven now, love. So I suppose it's time to move on.'

'Yes but what would Dad say about that Trevor though?' Herbert asked. 'I reckon he'd hate it if he knew he was here.'

17

'Oh I don't think so,' Mum replied. 'And will you stop calling Trevor 'That Trevor' please? It's awfully bad manners.'

'Yes but surely - '

'Surely your dad would be happy for me?' Mum said, completing her son's sentence. 'And you of course.'

'Yes but when Dad was alive it was so much fun and we used to go to the park and play cricket and go ice skating and - '

'We can still do all that,' Mum said, her eyes sparking up. 'With Trevor! In fact only yesterday he mentioned something about an international rugby match!'

'But it's always better if it's just us, Mum,' Herbert said, cracking a knuckle. 'And who wants to go to a rugby match anyway? That Trevor's a loser!'

'Hey now, don't you say that!' Mum shouted, crinkling up her forehead. 'It's mean and as I've said, stop saying 'That Trevor' – it's horrible.'

'What's going on?' Trevor asked, trotting down the stairs. 'Sorry, I got delayed on the toilet. I couldn't get my aim right, if you know what I mean!'

'Yes, great, let's call the newspapers,' Herbert barked, clenching his fists into tight little balls. Turning around, he sprinted out of the room, disappearing up the stairs.

'What've I done now?' Trevor asked, kissing Mum on the lips.

'Oh don't worry, he'll be fine,' Mum said, pressing into Trevor's round, muscular body. 'You know what he's like and anyway, these things take time. He still misses Rob, even after all these years.'

'I suppose he will do,' Trevor said, his lips breaking into a tiny smile. 'He's been through a lot, poor kid.'

THREE

After tea, Herbert, his mum and Trevor watched their favourite T.V. programme, Celebrity in the attic. 'What would you do if you were famous, Herbert?' Trevor asked, shoving an enormous biscuit into his mouth.

I'd banish you to Jupiter, Herbert thought, glancing at Trevor's fat, unshaven face.

'Come on, Herb,' Trevor repeated.

'Err, I don't know,' Herbert replied, shrugging his shoulders.

'I'd have my hair done by Derek Boyles, that top stylist in London,' Mum said, caressing her blonde locks. 'And I'd buy a Range Rover Sport and I'd have my teeth whitened and - '

'I've got a tin of white paint in my garage,' Trevor exclaimed. 'I could whiten your teeth for nothing!'

A wild, hearty laugh escaped from his mouth. His fat body rattled up and down on the sofa, almost sliding off the edge. Mum couldn't stop herself. She joined in with Trevor's rib-tickling laughter.

Herbert clamped his lips shut, pressing them together. *You're about as funny as a broken leg,* he thought. But Trevor wouldn't stop.

'Come on Herbert,' he shouted, drawing a glass of red wine to his lips. 'You still haven't said anything!'

'Well let's face it,' Herbert said, folding his arms into a tight knot. 'I'm never going to be famous am I?'

'Why not?' Trevor asked.

'Because I'm not very good at anything, that's why.'

'Hey, don't say that,' Mum said, pursing her lips into a smile. 'Trevor said you played well in goals last week. And you've got your guitar! Well, when you remember to take it out of its case!'

'And you only let in seventeen goals,' Trevor shouted as a cheeky grin sprouted onto his lips. 'Very funny!' Herbert replied, staring at the carpet.

'You'd probably save more shots blindfolded, Herb!' Trevor said, rising to his feet. 'Anyway, target practice for me now - on the toilet! And if I don't score a bulls-eye this time, there'll be trouble!'

Mum laughed, shaking her thin head. Herbert remained tight lipped. 'He thinks he's so funny but obviously he's not,' Herbert said as Trevor climbed the stairs. 'He's just a born loser.'

'Oh just give him a chance, love,' Mum said, holding out her palms. 'And could you please stop calling him a loser? He's not all that bad.'

Jumping onto the floor, Herbert climbed onto his mum's cosy armchair, cuddling into her. He closed his eyes, burying his head into her pink pyjamas. 'Yes he is, Mum,' he said. 'He's about as funny as a car crash. Why can't he just crawl into a hole and disappear forever or even better, be *in* a car crash?'

Mum peeled her son away from her. 'That's a horrible thing to say!' she barked, grabbing hold of his wrists. 'Don't you *ever* talk like that again about Trevor, got it?'

'But why can't it just be the two of us?' Herbert asked as his mum tightened her grip. Tears dampened his eyes as he struggled to break free. 'It's well better when it's just us! We don't need him around and you *know* it!'

The skin on Mum's face lost its fresh, healthy glow. The sparkle in her eyes vanished. Her forehead creased up, its tight skin packed together like a closed concertina. Still holding onto Herbert's wrists, she gazed into his eyes.

'I've told you, Herbert!' she said. 'I don't want to be on my own for the rest of my life! And anyway, without Trevor, you'd have been in that after school club today and you hate that!'

'But - '

'Never mind your buts! Sometimes, you're just unbelievably selfish. One day, you might realise just how lucky you are. And you'll start to appreciate all the things that we BOTH do for you! Now go and sit over there, I've had enough of you. You're a selfish little brat!'

She released her grip. Herbert's body fell backwards, landing softly on the thick rug. Switching his ears off, Herbert trotted across the room. He climbed onto a leather chair in the corner.

Dropping his head, he closed his eyes, conjuring up an image. His dad's face appeared in the dark but comforting blackness. Herbert's mind transported him to the local park.

It was a warm, spring day. A gentle breeze was blowing, pushing lonely, dusty leaves along the path. Herbert clutched a plastic cricket bat. His dad bowled a ball to him. His mum, standing close, held out her arms, ready to catch it.

Together, his mum and dad laughed as Herbert missed the ball and toppled over. Herbert clambered to his feet. He dragged the bat behind him, giggling like a clown's apprentice.

I wish things were the way they used to be, Dad, he thought. *I loved those days and if I could turn back the clock, I'd -*

But you can't, Son, his dad whispered from a hidden, heavenly place. *You have to live in the present...*

Can you do me a favour, Dad? Herbert asked. *Can you get rid of that Trevor for me? Mum doesn't really like him. He's just a stupid, fat loser who thinks he's so funny and -*

'I'm calling the police!' Trevor shouted out. He marched into the lounge, his slippers bouncing up and down. The images in Herbert's mind suddenly disappeared. Herbert prized open his eyelids, wiping his eyes with his fingertips.

'Why, what's up?' Mum asked.

'Somebody's stealing the toilet rolls,' Trevor replied. 'Or eating them! And it's not me because I only ever use one piece, even for a number two.'

Two lonely tears dripped out of Herbert's eyelids. He pulled himself up, wiping them away with his sleeve.

'What's wrong, Herb?' Trevor asked. 'Been looking in the mirror?'

Mum shot a sharp look of disapproval into Trevor's direction. Her eyes narrowed into little slits. 'He's all right,' she said, beckoning her son over. 'He's just missing his dad, aren't you love?'

Herbert climbed onto his mum's knee and once again, hugged into her.

Trevor disappeared into the kitchen. Soon, he returned, armed with a large glass, brimming over with sparkling lemonade. 'This'll do you the world of good, Herb,' he said.

'Thanks,' Herbert said, as a tiny smile appeared on his lips. Herbert's nose sniffled as he poured the cool liquid into his throat. Then, with one hand, he rubbed his eyes, his fingers prodding around his eyelids.

'Hey and don't you ever worry about being famous, Herbert,' Mum said to her son. 'Because I'll still love you the same whether you end up famous or not!'

'And your dad, of course,' Trevor added. 'I'm sure he's looking down on you now, as we speak!'

Peering deep into his mum's eyes, Herbert nodded.

'I know he is,' he said, hugging her body. 'And one day, if I'm ever famous, I'll - '

'You will be famous one day, though, Herb,' Trevor shouted out, interrupting as usual. He slurped another mouthful of red wine from his glass before continuing.

'You might be in that Guinness book of records, for wearing the world's smelliest underpants!'

Trevor's mouth rattled out a raucous laugh, his teeth popping over his thick lips. 'At least my breath doesn't stink like a hippo's!' Herbert snapped. Closing his eyes, he buried his head into his mum's pyjamas once more.

Mum sent a razor sharp stare across the room. Her eyes turned into bright red lazer beams. 'I thought you were supposed to be trying,' she whispered.

Trevor rolled his eyes, puffing out a long blow. Raising his thick, muscular arms, he shrugged his shoulders. Then he tipped the remains of his wine into his mouth.

FOUR

Saturday morning arrived. 'Who's taking me to my football match, Mum?' Herbert asked. 'It's me this week, love,' his mum answered.

'Oh that's good,' Herbert said, stretching on his shin-pads. 'As long as it's not that Trevor again, the *un-funniest* man in the world.'

'Hey, I've told, haven't I?' It's Trevor thank you very much, not *that* Trevor,' Mum replied, dragging a brush through her tangled hair. 'And he's only trying his best Herbert, so can you please just give him a chance? For me, eh? And anyway, I always take you to your football.'

'It's just that last week - '

'I was at the hairdressers!'

'And the week before?'

'I was at Joanne's fortieth birthday lunch; with all the girls, remember? I can't be in two places at once but anyway, I've hardly missed a match all season!'

'Trevor was so embarrassing last week, Mum,' Herbert said, pulling a thick, blue football sock over a shin-pad. 'He was screaming and shouting and everybody was looking at him. And all he was talking about was how rugby's a real game and football's just for wimps and - '

'Oh he was probably just pulling your leg,' Mum chuckled.

'I know but if Dad was still alive, he'd - '

'Well he isn't, is he?' Mum said, her eyes frosting over. 'But he'll probably be sitting on a cloud somewhere, cheering you on, so come on – let's have a win for your dad!'

'Well Trevor just gets on my nerves with all that rugby stuff, Mum!'

'Oh come on, you know what he's like by now,' Mum said. 'He just loves winning!'

He's a loser more like, Herbert thought, puffing out a long, deflated pocket of air.

Mum planted a kiss on the top of her son's forehead, squeezing his head with her fingers. 'Well I think he should just stick to his rugby Mum,' Herbert said, 'because he knows nothing about football. He just *thinks* he does!'

'Now, now, love,' Mum said, glancing at the clock on the wall. 'That's a bit unfair. Trevor just wants you to win, that's all. Anyway, you won't be winning anything if we don't get a move on.'

Driving down the road, Mum's face exploded into a gigantic grin. 'Trevor said he's got a surprise for us later on!' she exclaimed.

'Why is he leaving the country?' Herbert snapped, cracking the tiny bones in his knuckles.

'Now stop that!' Mum barked, gripping the car's steering wheel. 'That's just not fair! Trevor's got feelings you know, just like you and me. So please, stop being so horrible to him.'

'But couldn't the police arrest him or something, for being the world's fattest man?'

Herbert snapped back. 'And lock him up in one of those padded cells and throw away the key?'

Mum pressed her foot hard on the car's brake pedal, pulling down her indicator lever. The car came to an abrupt halt at the side of the road. Herbert jerked forwards, the car's seatbelt pressing into his body.

'Do you know, that's a horrible thing to say, Herbert!' his mum shouted. 'I'm really surprised at you!'

'Well if Dad was alive, he'd punch Trevor in the face and sort him out and - '

'Oh don't start all that again,' Mum said, covering up her ears. 'I just can't take it anymore. You're driving me insane, love!'

Lowering her head, she gently head-butted the car's steering wheel, several times. Then she rested her forehead on its hard leather.

'It's just that Dad - '

'Herbert!' his mum screamed, digging her nails into the steering wheel's soft leather. 'Your dad died four years ago Love! So it's time to move on!'

'I know but Trevor - '

'Trevor's alright,' Mum barked. 'You've just got to get used to him. Anyway, if you had your way, I'd be on my own for the rest of my life.'

'But can't you find somebody else?'

'Who?' Mum asked. 'Any ideas? Should I email the Queen and see if she knows any rich princes?'

'You know what I mean, Mum,' Herbert said, staring out of the window. 'You can do better than that Trevor.'

'Will you STOP calling him THAT Trevor! Do that one more time and you're grounded! Just think about me for a change!'

'But - '

'No 'buts' Herbert! I'm thirty-five and I'm not getting any younger am I? Trevor treats me well *and* he makes me laugh. And listen, he

33

spends a lot of his *own* money on you too, so just pack all this nonsense in. I've had enough!'

'I know but - '

'One day Herbert, I'll tell you just how hard it's been! I'm walking around in rags at the moment or haven't you noticed? And it's because most of my money goes on you, Herbert, for your fancy tops and trainers and stuff. So just cut it out. And leave Trevor alone!'

An unhappy, frosty atmosphere, as silent as the moon's surface, settled on the car.

'Hopefully one day you'll realise,' Mum continued, tears flooding into her eyes.

'I'd just love things to be the way they were,' Herbert snapped. 'And this Trevor, well he'll never be my dad, even though he's beginning to think he is.'

'Trevor doesn't think he's your dad,' Mum barked, turning the car's ignition key. 'And he never will.'

The car's engine purred into life. Mum turned to her son, her soft fingers stroking his face. She gazed into his eyes, her tears squeezing out of her eyelids.

'Trevor's just trying his best, that's all. He'll never, ever replace your dad. Nobody will.'

A wry smile crackled onto Mum's lips. 'I know Trevor's not as funny as he thinks he is, but, well, perhaps that's why I like him so much. And he's a great big softie deep down and that's, well, kind of sweet to me.'

'But Dad's missed so much, Mum,' Herbert muttered. 'He would have loved to watch me playing footy and - '

'I know,' Mum interrupted, slicing her son's sentence in half. 'Life can be cruel sometimes. But we've just got to get on with our lives now.'

Herbert dabbed his tear filled eyes with his football shirt's light green sleeve.

'I'm sure your dad's watching you from heaven right now,' his mum added, leaning over to kiss her son. 'So let's make some great saves today – let's make your dad proud of you!'

'Well I'm asking Dad to send me a sign,' Herbert sniffed. 'I need to know that he's watching me.'

'And me of course!' Mum said, her eyes glazing over. 'Anyway, your dad might be an angel for all we know, fluttering those wings of his.'

Two tiny chuckles joined together, rising up into the air, defrosting the car's icy atmosphere. Mum rubbed her eyes with a small white handkerchief. She pressed the car's accelerator pedal down, smoothly moving up the road.

The car turned into the Vikings' football team's car park. 'Let's focus upon the game,' Mum said. 'It's fifty pence for every good save you make!'

36

'Hey it was a pound last week!' Herbert exclaimed.

'Was it?' his mum replied. 'Well I'll see what I can do. Anyway, it's nice to see you all happy again, so come on, let's get down to business! And remember, your dad's watching you too, so make sure you play well.'

'I will, Mum,' Herbert said, stretching his lips wide. He pushed open the car's door and sprinted away onto the field. Joining his teammates, he chased and kicked a ball around before standing in the wide mouth of the goals.

Mum lowered her head, resting her nose on the steering wheel's circular middle. She closed her eyes, listening to her faint, fragile breathing. A whiff of leather puffed up into her nostrils as she drifted off into silence.

'If you can hear me Rob,' she whispered, as tears poured from her eyes. 'Please help us. I love you, wherever you are. And I miss you so much that it hurts. Oh and if you could send our

Herbert a sign that'd be great. He's turning into a brilliant boy, you know, a son to be proud of. But I don't half worry about him sometimes…'

She peered through the car's dusty window, her eyes fixed onto her son's distinctive green and yellow goalkeeper's shirt.

Don't you worry, love, she thought, her damp, sapphire blue eyes lighting up like two bright sparklers. *You'll have a very happy life with me, I promise you…with or without Trevor.*

FIVE

As Herbert sorted out a mountain of football cards, the front door opened. Trevor marched in, carrying an enormous sports bag.

'Here we go, here we go, here we go!' he screamed, bursting into song. He ruffled up Herbert's hair, almost pushing him over. 'We whooped them, Herb!' he cried, throwing his bag down.

'Oh,' Herbert replied, staring at his cards. He looked at Trevor's fat, unshaven face. It was covered in sharp, brown stubble, covering his chubby chins like theatre make-up. A small, silver earring dangled from his earlobe and the shortest hair in the world sat on the top of his head.

As usual, a short-sleeved, red Rugby shirt was clinging to him, winning a world record for the tightest top in the world. Two thick arms hung out of its sleeves, covered in tattoos.

What on earth does that fat fool look like?
Herbert thought, stretching a rubber band
around a pile of cards. *He's a gorilla. All he needs is
a zoo and he'll be sorted.*

Trevor waltzed into the kitchen. 'What on
earth's up with Herb now?' he asked, kissing
Mum.

'Oh he's in one of those moods again,' she
said. 'You know what he's like. I think he's just
still missing his dad that's all. Maybe I'll send him
to a counsellor or something or ask the school
about a psychologist. I'll have a chat with Mr
Skelhorn as soon as I can.'

'Well he doesn't like me one little bit,'
Trevor said as he filled up the kettle. 'In fact, if I
was on fire, he'd walk straight past me and water
the plants before putting me out!'

'Oh don't be daft!' Mum chuckled,
wrapping her arms around Trevor's muscular
frame. 'Please don't say stuff like that – it's silly!'

Trevor pulled away from his girlfriend's tall, slim body, turning around to place the kettle onto its base. Mum smoothed her hands across his shoulders, rubbing into his muscles.

'To be honest, Suzanne, I've been having a good think and well, I'm not sure if I can go on like this,' Trevor announced, his voice quivering.

'I'm beginning to dread coming round. I've tried everything; even tickets for the footy match, which cost a fortune. But your Herbert doesn't like me one little bit.'

'He just needs time, that's all, Trevor,' Mum replied.

'Well I don't think he'll ever like me to be honest,' Trevor continued. 'So it might be, well, err; best to call it a day before everybody gets hurt. I'm sure you'll find somebody else, Suzanne. Perhaps somebody who your Herbert likes for a change.'

'Oh don't say all that,' Mum said. 'You're talking rubbish!'

She grabbed hold of Trevor's thick body, squeezing into it. Then she planted a gentle kiss onto his lips. 'Where would I be without you, eh?'

'Well we'll just have to see how it goes,' Trevor said, feigning a smile. 'I'm only human and I can only take so much. I've even been thinking of - '

Walking into the kitchen, Herbert dragged his feet, his head bowed. 'Have you cleaned your football boots, Herb?' Trevor asked.

'No I haven't!' Herbert snapped, opening up the refrigerator.

'I'll clean them for you if you like,' Trevor said, throwing out a big smile. 'I'll have them as good as new in no time!'

'I'm quite capable of doing them myself, thanks,' Herbert snarled, his sharp, rose thorn words pricking Trevor. He disappeared into the lounge, grunting like a wild boar. 'See what I mean, Suzanne?' Trevor said, running his hand over his scalp.

Staring out of the window, Trevor managed to stem the flow of tears building up behind his eyes. A thousand thoughts tumbled around his head, throwing his mind into chaos.

He placed two teabags into a small teapot and poured boiling water onto them. He watched them spin around in the swirling water as he drifted into a deep daydream.

'I'll have a word with him,' Mum said, her hands resting on her boyfriend's broad shoulders. As she massaged his muscles, she didn't notice Trevor's tear filled eyes. 'I'm sure he'll come round eventually,' she added. 'He just needs a little more time.'

'Well I hope so, Suzanne,' Trevor answered. 'Otherwise I might have to, well, err, you know, err, call it a day.'

'Oh don't say that,' Mum said as Trevor twisted his body around. She peered into his damp, misty eyes. 'Are you ok love?' she asked.

'Err, of course I am,' Trevor replied, scratching his eyes with two chunky fingertips. 'I just got a fly caught in my eyes, that's all.'

'One fly in both eyes, eh?' Mum remarked, arching her eyebrows. She stroked Trevor's face with a long index finger, staring into him.

'My Herbert's the most precious thing in the world,' she whispered. 'But so are you, remember, so we'll work through all this together...'

'Well as I've said, I can't take much more, Suzanne,' Trevor mumbled, staring at the floor.

'And I mean it. The atmosphere when your Herbert's around's making me ill almost. I feel as wanted as a football at a rugby match. So, well, perhaps it's better just being on our own.'

'But we can't throw in the towel that easily,' Mum replied, lifting Trevor's spongy chin.

Her eyes locked onto Trevor's, gazing into his spirit. 'I'll work on him. And I'll ask the school about the counselling too. How's that, eh?'

'Well we'll have to see, Suzanne,' Trevor said, turning around to pull open the refrigerator's door. 'Because I can't go on like this for much longer.'

Herbert's mum slid out of the kitchen and into the lounge. Two tears pushed out of her eyes, sliding down her flushed up cheeks.

Wiping them away with her sleeve, she dropped down into her chair. She glanced over to her son, slumped in his seat, his eyes lost in the depths of his iPad.

Trevor looked out of the kitchen window, armed with a hot mug of tea, a digestive biscuit and a huge plateful of thoughts.

SIX

Around the dining table, Trevor revealed his surprise. 'Well it's brightening up out there,' he said, biting into a huge piece of beef. 'So it's a good job I've got these.'

He pulled three crumpled up wristbands out of his shirt pocket, holding them up in the air. 'They're for that travelling fairground that's on Parker's field,' he announced.

'I don't really like roller coasters,' Herbert said, not lifting up his head. 'I'm scared of heights, so what's the point in going?'

'Well there's always the 'Tea cups', Herb!' Trevor chuckled.

'And I'm sure there'll be plenty of other rides to choose from, love,' Mum added.

'I do like the dodgems,' Herbert said, pronging a chip with his fork. 'And the Waltzers!'

'They're only for wimps, Herb,' Trevor chuckled. 'Just like football!'

Mum kicked Trevor's leg, shooting an 'I thought you were supposed to be trying' look across the table.

'But, err, I do like watching football though,' Trevor added, rolling his eyes. 'I played a bit when I was younger. I used to play left back…left back in the changing rooms!'

A hearty laugh escaped from Trevor's mouth. Mum chuckled. But her son remained silent, surveying the food left on his plate.

'I do like the dodgems though!' Trevor exclaimed. 'In fact, a friend of mine went on the dodgems once, Herb,' he beamed, twisting his lips into a cheeky smile. 'And the police arrested him for dangerous driving!'

A long, raucous laugh rolled off Trevor's tongue. His whole body rattled up and down in the usual way. Herbert banged down a hard fist onto table. 'Your jokes are stupid!' he barked, standing up. He strutted out of the dining room and disappeared upstairs.

47

Herbert dived onto his bed, his body rising and falling like a beach ball. Picking up his fountain pen, he pulled out his journal. He scribbled out a letter, his pen dancing across the page:

Hello Dad,

I played well today against the Dragons! I even saved a penalty. But I wish you could have been there to watch me play. Anyway, don't forget that favour, Dad. I don't like Mum's new boyfriend, Trevor, one little bit. He thinks rugby is better than football, he thinks he's funny when he's not and when he takes his shoes off, his feet stink.

PLEASE can you get rid of him for me?

I love you, Dad and miss you lots and lots and lots.

P.S. Don't forget to send me that sign, if you can.

Love you loads, H xxx

Downstairs, in hushed tones, Herbert's mum chatted to her boyfriend:

'You'll have to try a lot harder than that, Trevor,' she snapped, shaking her head. She dipped a chocolate biscuit into her tea. Glazing over, her eyes stared out, lost in the flames of the gas fire.

'That's the problem, Suzanne,' Trevor said, running his index finger around the rim of his mug. 'I honestly don't know what else I can do. I've tried everything. But your Herbert doesn't like me – one little bit.'

A cold, biting wind blew across the table, freezing up their tongues. Trevor looked one way. Mum looked the other. Sitting in silence, they both tossed unhappy thoughts around, wondering about their futures.

Later on, Mum popped her head around the door. 'What's the book?' she asked.

'Err, just a new one from school,' Herbert replied, shutting his journal with a bang. 'It's just a little bit of homework that I forgot about.'

'Well hurry up and jump into the shower and put your pyjamas on,' she said, thrusting her hands onto her hips. 'We're going to the funfair in the morning, remember.'

'Do we have to go, Mum? Couldn't we go on our own next week?'

'Oh don't start all this again,' Mum groaned, standing over her son's bed.

'Trevor's already bought the tickets.'

'Can't we go to the museum instead?' Herbert asked.

'No we can't!' Mum barked, stamping he foot. 'Trevor's paid a lot of money for those wristbands, almost £50 I think.'

Herbert turned over, burying his head into his pillow. 'Well I'd rather go to the museum,' he muttered. 'It's much more interesting that a stupid old funfair.'

'Can you just be grateful for once?' his mum yelled as small veins protruded out of her neck. Kneeling down beside her son's bed, she moved her mouth close to her son's ear, whispering into it.

'You're driving me mad and you're starting to drive Trevor away as well!'

That's the best news I've heard in ages! Herbert thought, lying still. 'But can't I just stay at Grandma's instead?' he asked. 'You'll have a great time on your own with him.'

'No you can't!' Mum snapped, her piercing voice splitting the air. 'And Trevor's got a name too, it's not *'him'*. And look at me when I'm talking to you! It's not ALL about you, you know. What about me, eh?

'Yes I know, but - '

'Listen to me for a change! Trevor's fed up of all this bickering. If things don't work out at the funfair, well, we might never see him again.'

'Oh great, my prayers are working then,' Herbert shouted, screwing up his face.

'Why you ungrateful little - '

Mum's eyes turned a nasty shade of blood red. She raised her arm in the air, holding her open palm over her son's face. Herbert clamped his eyes shut. But nothing happened. 'Now get in that shower!' she screamed. 'And then it's straight to bed. Give Trevor a chance for heaven's sake!'

The bedroom door slammed with a big bang, rocking the doorframe. Mum bounced down the stairs like a wild buffalo, her feet almost breaking the wooden steps. Herbert rolled over, clutching his precious journal. The sudden sound of shouting drifted up the stairs. Tears poured out of Herbert's eyes, soaking into his pillow. And he sobbed and sobbed.

SEVEN

Wandering around the bustling fairground, Herbert, his mum and Trevor digested all the sights, sounds and smells. 'What should we go on first?' Herbert asked, dashing towards a twisting racetrack. 'These go-carts look good!'

Trevor pulled Mum to one side, tugging at her smart, green coat. 'Don't tell your Herbert but I hate roller coasters really,' he whispered. 'And to be honest, I'm a bit like Herbert in a way. I'm terrified of heights.'

'You must be joking!' Mum exclaimed, tickling Trevor's chest. 'A big strong rugby player like you, afraid of heights?'

'I only said I loved roller coasters to impress your Herbert!' Trevor replied.

'Don't be daft!' Herbert's mum giggled, flashing her whiter than white teeth.

'I knew I shouldn't have told you,' Trevor said, shoving his hands deep into his jeans' pockets. 'Anyway, don't tell Herbert whatever you do. If he thinks I'm a wimp, well, I suppose I might as well go home now.'

'Your secret's safe with me,' Mum chuckled, grabbing her boyfriend's hand.

'What secret?' Herbert asked, trotting back.

'Oh nothing,' Mum chortled.

Striding forwards, Trevor marched on ahead. Herbert and his mum linked arms, chatting as they skipped along. 'Just give him a chance,' she said. 'Without Trevor, we wouldn't even be here. So think about that!'

'But we could have come on our own though.'

'I couldn't afford it on my own,' Mum replied.

Soon, Trevor chanced upon a hand painted sign outside a small, beige tent. 'Hey, this looks interesting!' he shouted as rays of sunlight caressed his face. 'I've always been interested in this sort of stuff. Anybody fancy it?'

Herbert and his mum stared at the sign as Trevor read it out in a funny, American style accent. An unexpected giggle sprung up in the depths of Herbert's stomach as he tuned into Trevor's 'announcer' style voice.

Soon, the giggle grew into a loud laugh, bursting through Herbert's lips.

'The marvellous, magical and mysterious

Madame Mistral

I predict your future and I'm always correct

A bargain at only £5.00 per session

Family ticket just £20

Dogs and cats £2.00

Rabbits £1.00

Hamsters just 50p

Egyptian mummies FREE!

Booking fee only £5.00'

'Oh all that's a load of old rubbish, love,' Mum remarked, turning around. 'Come on Trevor, let's go and find the Donkey derby'.

'Aw yes, I love the Donkey derby!' Herbert exclaimed.

'Hey, do you know what the donkeys get for their lunch on Blackpool beach?' Trevor chuckled, displaying his protruding teeth like a squirrel.

'Carrots?' Mum asked.

'No!' Trevor cried. 'What about you Herb, do you know?'

'Err, apples and bananas?'

'Twenty minutes!' Trevor roared, his belly rattling out a rib-busting laugh. 'Oh I love that joke!'

Herbert squeezed his lips together, pushing a laugh back into his belly. He dropped his head, gazing at the ground. He avoided Trevor's grinning face, laughing like a lottery winner.

Mum forced out a laugh. 'That's the worst joke I've ever heard, love!' she giggled.

Trevor plunged his hands deep into his pockets, pulling out a crumpled up twenty pound note. 'Anyway, I think we should go in and see this Madame Mistral woman,' he announced. 'It's a laugh, isn't it Herb?'

A tiny smile parted Herbert's lips. 'Well she might tell me I'll be famous one day,' he said. 'And she might even tell us something about Dad, so yes, why not?'

'Well I'm not going in,' Mum retorted, folding her arms into a tight knot. 'If you believe in all that rubbish, you need your head testing!'

'Oh come on,' Trevor shouted, winking at Mum. 'Herbert WANTS to go in, don't you?'

A cheeky, persuading smile stretched Herbert's lips. 'Well if you think about it, Mum, she might even reveal some of Trevor's secrets,' he said. 'Well I suppose once won't do me any harm,' Mum replied.

She followed Trevor and Herbert down a twisting gravel path, strolling into a spacious tent. 'This thing's like a maze!' Trevor exclaimed, leading them down a narrow passageway. 'Where do we go next?'

He twisted his head, scanning his searchlight eyes around. 'Oh here we go,' Trevor said, following a black arrow, crudely painted onto a thick piece of cardboard. 'Good job I've got my Boy scout's directions badge!'

EIGHT

They stopped inside a large, grassy space. Thick beams of golden sunlight squeezed through an open dome at the top, bathing the tent in warm, bright light.

A round table stood in the middle of the tent, carved from a single piece of ancient oak. It was standing on a large, crimson rug, its silver edges frayed with age.

Scattered around the table were four matching chairs, their seats covered in a red, patterned material. On the table's dull surface, a crystal ball rested on an ornate wooden stand. Surrounding it was a collection of cards, teabags and gemstones.

An old woman, short in stature, suddenly appeared. She walked through a long, lilac curtain, its material covered in a swarm of silvery stars. Hobbling along on an old, wooden crutch, she dragged her slippers through the grass.

Wrapped around her head was a tight, yellow headband, with four different rubies set into an ornate silver clasp on the front. Long dyed brown hair, tinged with streaks of gold, framed her wrinkle-infested face. Deep, dark shadows lay under her eyes, hanging still like silent, sleeping slugs.

A long, crooked nose was standing to attention in the middle of her ancient face. Several stray hairs protruded out of its nostrils, like tiny, silver springs. Enormous bronze earrings swung from her ears, dangling down in a perfect, symmetrical line.

'It's your mum in a few years' time, Herb!' Trevor chuckled, nudging into Herbert's arm.

Herbert pushed out a long sigh, turning his eyes towards the old lady.

Madame Mistral peered at everybody. Her old, wise eyes burned bright like two hot sparklers on bonfire night.

'I will tell you what is going to happen to you all today,' she announced in a strange, foreign voice. 'But for an extra tenner, I'll predict your futures…for the rest of your lives!'

As he cleared his throat, Trevor handed Madame Mistral his twenty-pound note. 'Err, just the standard family ticket thanks,' he said, pulling up a chair. Herbert and his mum joined him.

'Err, what's the booking fee for?' Trevor asked.

Madame Mistral stretched her shadowy eyes. She nodded her head, sucking in a long, deep breath. 'Tea bags are very expensive these days, my friend.'

She spread out a small set of colourful cards across the table. They circled her smooth, crystal ball in a perfect arch. Then she ripped open a teabag, sprinkling the contents over the cards.

Opening up a silver box, engraved with a Celtic, interlocking pattern, she pulled out a small brown object. She stared hard at it, resting in between the deep lines of her palm.

'This ancient dragon's bone was discovered by Arkhad,' Madame Mistral said. 'A famous Celtic wizard who roamed this land many moons ago.'

Rolling the bone in between two flat palms, she gently massaged it. She pulled her hands apart, gazing at her precious treasure.

'Arkhad's bone has the power to unlock the doors to your futures, my friends. Trust the power of Arkhad and incredible happiness will be yours!'

'Well let's get on with it,' Trevor interrupted, shrugging his wide shoulders. 'I've got a dodgem to catch.'

Madame Mistral gazed at Mum, her fiery eyes drilling into her forehead. Then she turned over a card. 'Oh dear,' she said, twirling the card in her fingers. 'You will always have to work hard in life, my friend. But one day you will be rewarded.'

'Well I sort of know all that already,' Mum huffed, rolling her eyes.

Madame Mistral peered into her crystal ball. Her eyeballs rotated as she plunged into another world. She ran her fingers over the ball's smooth, glass surface. A dazzling beam of light suddenly appeared, surrounding the ball and lighting up Madame Mistral's face.

The old lady's wrinkles seemed to disappear. The light pierced her facial skin, somehow transforming her into a pretty young woman.

'Hey, I'm not having that!' Trevor said, nudging Herbert's mum. 'It's obviously some sort of trick with the lights!'

Rocking her head from side to side, Madame Mistral closed her eyes, her young, unblemished face still bathed in the bright, golden light. She raised her arms, her fingers dancing in the air.

'Oh dear!' she screamed, opening up her eyes. The ball's strange light source vanished. Madame Mistral's old, wrinkled face reappeared. Her wispy breathing stopped. Clasping a hand over her mouth, Madame Mistral stared deep into Mum's eyes.

'DANGER!' she yelled. 'YOU'RE ALL IN GREAT DANGER!'

Everybody stared at the old lady, their jaws dropping open like silent puppets. 'Beware of a silver screw, an old hunter, aniseed rock and thirty five red balloons.'

'Thanks for that,' Mum hissed, cracking open a tiny smile. 'I'll be *very* careful!'

Madame Mistral stroked her pointed chin. 'What is your favourite animal by the way?'

'Oh, err, I don't know,' Mum replied. 'It's probably a Golden eagle.'

'That's a bird, my friend, not an animal,' Madame Mistral said. 'But that'll do, I suppose.'

'Well I've always wanted to fly,' Mum said. 'I'd love a go in one of those giant hot air balloons.'

Madame Mistral closed her eyes. 'Arkhad's telling me he'll -'

'Hey, there's a lot of hot air around here,' Trevor shouted, wafting his palm around his nose. 'Somebody's let Polly out of her cage. And it absolutely stinks!'

Whilst his mum shook her head, Herbert's lips parted and an explosive laugh escaped. *Now that WAS funny!* he thought, catching Trevor's gaze. Mum joined in too, giggling as if somebody was tickling her feet with a feather.

'That smell is your breath, my friend,' Madame Mistral remarked, her razor sharp words cutting into Trevor's skin. 'Have you ever heard of a toothbrush?'

'Hey, I brushed my teeth this morning,' Trevor replied. 'And I used that floss stuff and mouthwash and - '

'Well as I was *going* to say before I was so *rudely* interrupted,' Madame Mistral continued, turning towards Herbert's mum. 'Arkhad will assist you, my friend. If your wish is to fly like a Golden eagle, then so be it!'

Madame Mistral closed her eyes, falling into a deep, hypnotic trance. Her head swayed from side to side as she chanted a magic spell. 'Blah, bling, blon, Dlah, dling, dlon. Tlah, tling, tlon, is the kettle on?'

Mum couldn't help it. Another giggle stretched her lips, displaying her neat, polished teeth. She covered her mouth with a hand. Madame Mistral banged her fist hard onto the table.

'NEVER mock the power of Arkhad!' she yelled, twisting her face into a mass of long, deep wrinkles. 'Or you will regret it! For the rest of your days!'

NINE

'What about me then?' Trevor asked, running a fat hand over his scalp. Madame Mistral picked up Arkhad's bone. Placing it in her palm, she clasped her bony fingers around it.

'Your time will come, my friend,' she said, blowing onto her hand. 'But first, you must learn the power of patience.'

Madame Mistral turned over two cards. A monstrous dragon and a fierce looking pirate stared out at her. She dropped the bone onto the table. It rolled around until it stopped next to a teabag. 'Ah, always the joker, I see,' she said.

'That's me,' Trevor answered, forcing his lips into a grin. 'And probably the most popular man in the rugby -'

'The crystal ball is telling me something,' Madame Mistral snapped, cutting Trevor's sentence into two. 'You're about as popular as a rattlesnake in a lucky dip, my friend. And *somebody* around this table doesn't like you one little bit!' All eyes narrowed, glancing into each other's faces.

Moving his chair around, Trevor didn't answer. He tapped his chunky fingers on the table, staring at the damp blades of grass beneath him. Herbert lowered his head, avoiding Madame Mistral's eyes. He clenched his fists under the table, tensing up his toes. Then he sucked in a large pocket of air, filling his lungs.

How on earth does she know that? Herbert thought. *And even Madame Mistral thinks Trevor's a plonker. You can tell a mile off.*

Rocking to and fro, Madame Mistral started to hum a strange melody. Then she peered into Trevor's eyes, her strong, concentrated gaze almost knocking him off his chair.

'Your aura* is full of blacks and blues,' she announced. 'Those dark but powerful colours are always a sign of a deep sadness, perhaps an unfinished business, from long, long ago.'

Coughing and spluttering, Trevor covered his mouth with his hand. Soon his face was as white as a ghoul. His eyes zipped around in their sockets. He shuffled around in his chair, rotating his big bottom.

'Err, I'm very happy thanks, Madame Mistral,' he mumbled. 'But well, err, it's difficult at times, especially if people don't like me.'

Still drumming his fingers on the table's polished surface, Trevor glanced at Herbert. 'Then just be yourself,' Madame Mistral remarked, her voice raising its pitch.

She fixed her sharp gaze onto Trevor, her wise, old eyes delving into his spirit. 'Trying too hard, or even worse, trying to be somebody else, almost always ends in disaster, my friend.'

Trevor rubbed his eyes with his fingers, throwing out another loud, throaty cough.

'You're holding onto your painful past,' Madame Mistral announced. 'I can see shadows of sadness floating around your aura*. So let go, my friend. You can never turn back the hands of time; no matter how hard you try. But you can always learn from what has happened...'

'Err, yes, I sort of know what you mean,' Trevor stuttered, glancing up at Herbert once more.

'What is your favourite animal, by the way?'

'Oh it's got to be an orang-utan,' Trevor answered, his voice more upbeat. 'Imagine swinging around all day *and* being allowed to scratch your bum without anybody looking at you funny. Oh I'd love a bit of that!'

'Well Arkhad will assist you, my friend,' Madame Mistral said, sliding Arkhad's bone across the table. 'If that is your wish, then so be it!'

Once more, Madame Mistral plunged into a deep sleep, chanting out another magic spell. 'Blingo, Mingo, Tingo, Gingo, Dingle, Dongle, Donazoo, Blongo, Mongo, Tongo, Gongo, I'm dying for a brew!'

She pulled open her eyes, poking the little bone with that same, bony index finger.

'Oh dear,' she announced. 'Beware of the number thirteen. It's unlucky for some, my friend, but VERY unlucky for you. Today, in fact, so Arkhad's tells me. And I see a duck called Brian, whatever that means.'

'Oh right,' Trevor mumbled, chewing at his thumbnail.

---

* A person's aura is a colourful field of subtle radiation surrounding a person. It is invisible. However, some spiritual people claim to be able to see them.

TEN

Herbert peered through his thick glasses. He focussed upon Madame Mistral's wrinkles, stretching across her face like tiny, intersecting railway lines. Her eyes turned towards him, their incredible brightness almost hypnotising him.

'Can you help me too, please, Mrs Mistral?' he asked.

'It's not my fault you're ugly, I'm afraid, Herbert,' she replied. 'And its *not* Mrs, it's Madame, but anyway, I'll see what secrets Arkhad is willing to reveal for you…'

'Hey, who are you calling ugly, Madame Mistral?' Trevor barked, sitting upright.

'Sometimes, the truth hurts my friend,' Madame Mistral replied. 'Take a long, hard look in the mirror.'

'Hey Mistral!' Mum shouted out. 'We've not come here to be insulted!'

'Don't worry, my friend,' Madame Mistral said, clutching Mum's hand. 'It's just my silly sense of humour, that's all. I'm sure Herbert will find a girlfriend when he's older. As long as he has a head transplant!'

'Hey stop that,' Trevor yelled, standing up. 'Your jokes are stupid and you're getting on everybody's nerves.'

'At long last, Trevor!' Madame Mistral announced. 'You can finally see your own reflection in the mirror.'

'I've just thought,' Herbert asked, squashing his eyelids together. 'How do you know my name?'

'Hey and mine,' Trevor added.

'You're all forgetting *one* very important thing,' Madame Mistral remarked, pushing a teabag across the table. 'Arkhad tells me everything!'

'As if!' Trevor cried, shaking his head.

'I see a white ball shaped like an egg, tucked under your arm,' Madame Mistral said, her voice sharp and low. 'I see a red rugby shirt and an important cup match.'

'How on earth do you know that?' Trevor asked, swallowing up his words. 'Will we win?'

'Be strong and believe in yourself!' Madame Mistral shouted out. 'And nothing will come between you and your dreams!'

'So what's my name, then?' Mum asked, not wanting to be missed out.

'Now you're a difficult one, my dear,' Madame Mistral replied, gazing into Herbert's mum's eyes. 'I'll ask Arkhad and tell you later. But first, let's look into Herbert's future…'

Madame Mistral gathered up her precious bone. She stroked it, cupping it in her hands. Closing her eyes, she chanted her mysterious, magical words once more. 'Hig, Hag, Hugars, Tig, Tag, Tugars, Zig, Zag, Zugars, Milk and two sugars!'

She let the bone slide out of her hands. It landed with a thud on the table, rolling around before coming to a stop. A gentle smile spread across her lips as she scooped it up. Madame Mistral sprinkled the contents of the ripped teabag over her set of cards.

'Now let me see,' she whispered, running her fingers through the tea leaves.

The tent was as silent as stone. Madame Mistral peered into her crystal ball, her skeletal hands gliding over its smooth glass once more.

'Is your name Herbert Humphries?' she asked.

'Wow, how do you know that?' Trevor exclaimed.

'Silence, you big lump!' Madame Mistral retorted, pushing the bone into the cards.

'Hey, the last person who called me a 'big lump' ended up in hospital!' Trevor yelled, raising his bottom lip. 'And I don't mean visiting.'

Madame Mistral turned towards him. She fell silent, sucking in a long breath of air.

'Please remember what I've already said, my friend,' she remarked. 'Just be yourself! And as sure as summer following spring, success and happiness will follow your footsteps. Wherever you choose to tread…'

'I know but - '

'Just listen to the wise, whisperings of your heart, Trevor!' Madame Mistral added. 'And be quiet now please. Arkhad's telling me Herbert's secrets.'

Once more she closed her eyes, humming that same, strange melody. She rocked her whole body to and fro, falling into a deep, hypnotic trance. Trevor grinned out a hearty smile. 'That tea she drinks must be strong,' he whispered to Mum.

Soon, Madame Mistral's eyes opened. She ran her fingertips over the backs of her cards. She picked one up, turning it over. An 'upside down' face stared out at her, dressed in regal clothes from the past. 'The 'hanging' Duke,' she said, nodding her head. '*Very* interesting.'

Her fingers moved across the table's surface. She picked up Arkhad's bone, clasping it in her hand. Then she let go of it, dropping it onto the table. Picking up another card, she let out a powerful scream. She held the card close to her chest, her fingers trembling.

'Danger!' she shrieked, rocking her chair to and fro.

Her chair lost its balance, toppling over on its back legs. Collapsing into a heap, Madame Mistral rolled around in the grass. Still clutching the card, she cackled like a wild and withered witch.

'The 'Devilish demon'' she cried out, holding the bent card in front of her eyes. 'Herbert's in great danger and it's all going to happen today!'

ELEVEN

'Why, what's up?' Herbert's asked.

'Nothing's up,' Madame Mistral moaned. 'Well not yet anyway.'

Pulling herself up, Madame Mistral sucked in a long, deep breath. 'Your secret wish is about to come true,' she exclaimed, looking towards Herbert. 'You're going to become world famous. And it's all going to happen before the end of this very afternoon!'

An ear-splitting laugh pushed its way out of Trevor's mouth. 'Pull the other one,' he chuckled. 'I mean, how can anybody become world famous in a *day*?'

'Arkhad never lies, my friend,' Madame Mistral cried.

'But what about the danger part?' Herbert asked, cracking his knuckles.

Madame Mistral stared into Herbert's glazed eyes, her gaze almost melting his glasses.

'Sometimes, the Devilish demon follows those who dream of being famous, Herbert,' she said. 'But don't worry, my friend. Conquer your fear of heights and the path to fame could be yours.'

Herbert's eyes grew bigger as he stared into the old lady's eyes. 'Err, well, I'll try my best, Madame Mistral,' he stuttered.

'Tell you what, Herb,' Trevor interrupted. 'If you're brave enough to go on the 'Big wheel', I'll buy you those expensive trainers you're always going on about!'

'Thanks,' Herbert replied, his mind throwing up an instant thought. *But I'd rather wait until Mum buys them for me, thanks.*

'The 'Valdorama' is the most famous Ferris wheel in the world, my friends,' Madame Mistral announced, rolling Arkhad's bone between her fingers.

'I said a Big wheel,' Trevor chuckled, 'not a blooming Ferris wheel, whatever that is!'

'The Ferris wheel IS the Big wheel, you dimwit!' Madame Mistral barked, puffing out a long, loud blow. Trevor dragged his big body out of his chair. 'Hey, the last person who called me a 'dimwit' ended up needing seventeen stitches!'

'Why?' Madame Mistral remarked. 'Was he sewing up your lips to stop your tedious talking?'

'Hey, you cheeky - ' Trevor bawled.

'Oh, everybody just calm down,' Mum shouted. 'Anyway, it's time to go. I've had enough of all this lot!'

'She started it!' Trevor snapped, pointing at Madame Mistral's frail frame.

'No I didn't, Madame Mistral replied. 'I think you'll find you did, my friend.'

'Stop calling me your friend!' Trevor screamed, the whites of his eyes bulging out of their sockets. 'And I didn't start anything - you did!'

'Yes you did…my friend!'

'Stop it!' Herbert shouted, stretching out his arms. 'Just grow up, the lot of you!'

'Some people never grow up, Herbert,' Madame Mistral said, 'but Arkhad's telling me this - you will all GO up. Today in fact, in a few hours' time.'

'I'd love to meet this Arkhad fella,' Trevor exclaimed, punching his fist into a cupped hand. 'He deserves a bunch of fives!'

Madame Mistral didn't say anything. Fishing up Arkhad's bone, she trapped it in between her fingers. Then she rolled it over the tops of her cards.

'Arkhad's telling me to go to the toilet or I might wet myself,' she said. 'So I'll finish off with one final question for Herbert. What is your favourite animal?'

'Oh, err, it's probably a bat,' Herbert replied. 'I just love how they -'

'I've had enough of all this nonsense,' Mum interrupted, standing up. 'Come on, I'm off. What a waste of time *and* money!'

'If your wish is to hang around like a bat, then so be it!' Madame Mistral cried, her voice cutting through the noisy fuss.

Everybody stood up. Picking up Arkhad's bone once more, Madame Mistral climbed back onto her chair. 'Sit down, everybody,' she yelled. 'I haven't finished yet!'

'You're about as nutty as a bag of peanuts,' Trevor shouted.

'Arkhad has spoken, my friends,' Madame Mistral cried. 'You are all in *grave* danger, especially Harriet!'

'Who's Harriet?' Herbert asked.

'Oh she must have been in before you,' Madame Mistral answered. 'Herbert, I mean.'

'Oh this is just silly!' Mum snapped. 'Come on, let's go.'

Madame Mistral bayed like a donkey. Throwing her arms up into the air, she closed her eyes, tossing her head around. Her voice boomed out, loud, sharp and powerful. 'Hand me another tenner for the ancient spell of Professor Proctor's protection.'

'You'll need police protection in a minute,' Trevor barked, kicking his chair over. Grabbing the edge of the table, Trevor pushed it with great force. It tipped up and Madame Mistral's collection of objects scattered out all over the grass.

The crystal ball rolled off, crashing into the ground below. Trevor kicked it across the grass. Then he picked up its stand and threw it at against the side of the tent. 'You're a rip off, Mistral,' he yelled. 'All you're after is our money!'

'You'll all have to leave. Right now!' Madame Mistral screamed. 'Arkhad's reminding me about the toilet and I'm bursting!'

'Yes, and I bet your purse is bursting too!' Trevor retorted. 'And what if we don't want to leave? What will you do then, eh?'

'Well I'll probably wet myself and the stench will knock you out,' Madame Mistral replied. 'Unless you ask me for Wizard Warlock's 'Defence against Madame Mistral's wet knickers' spell.'

'Oh this is stupid,' Mum snapped as she pushed over a chair. 'I told you at the start it'd be a waste of money. The woman's obviously sick, Trevor.'

'Yes, sick of you lot!' Madame Mistral cried, kneeling down in the grass. 'You'll all be doomed if you walk out of my tent without protection!' She fished up her objects one by one, stuffing them into the pockets of her fading, flowery dress.

'If any of you dares to walk out of this fairground before the clock strikes five, then the angel of unfortunate events will come searching

85

for you,' she screamed. 'And Trevor, here's a warning. Don't let go of your big banana, whatever you do!'

'You're barmy!' Mum barked. 'You're nothing but a liar and a cheat!'

Madame Mistral's voice clicked into overdrive. She screamed out one final instruction, scrunching up her face. 'For an extra twenty pounds, I can cast the spell of Doctor Dressler's defence against helium balloons!'

'More money! You're nothing but a fake!' Mum yelled. 'And the cost keeps going up!'

'You will soon go up too, Suzanne,' Madame Mistral added. 'Now get out of my tent…before it's too late!'

TWELVE

'Hey, how do you know my name?' Mum asked, standing to attention.

'Arkhad told me,' Madame Mistral replied. 'He tells me everything.'

'Well I reckon it's just a lucky guess,' Mum snapped, her jaws shutting together like an attacking shark. She dashed over to Madame Mistral, pushing into her body.

Falling to her knees, she searched through the grass until she found Arkhad's bone. 'I'm taking this thing home with me,' Mum bawled. 'It might bring us a bit of luck for a change!'

'Nooooo!' Madame Mistral screamed, scrambling to her feet. 'Steal Arkhad's bone and the goddess of true love will fly away. *Never* to return.'

'Well hard luck, I'm keeping it!' Mum retorted. 'Let's just call it my souvenir!'

'Nooooo!' Madame Mistral yelled out once more, her screams punching the tent's canvas. Herbert was just about to ask his mum to return the bone when Trevor beat him to it.

'Come on, love,' he said. 'Give Madame Mistral her bone back. I suppose it belongs to her at the end of the day.'

'No, I'm keeping it!' Mum barked.

'I know, but that's stealing, Mum,' Herbert pleaded, stretching his eyelids.

'Herbert's right, Suzanne,' Trevor said, holding out his hand. 'It might be bad luck.'

'Oh this is a joke!' Mum shouted, banging the bone into her boyfriend's palm. Trevor passed the precious artefact to Herbert.

'You're a great lad, Herb, thinking of other people first – well done you,' he said.

Dashing towards Madame Mistral, Herbert bent down, placing Arkhad's bone into her palm. Then he helped her to pick up her strange collection of objects.

'You have a good heart, Herbert and your psychic channel is tuned into the seventh dimension,' the fortune teller whispered, still crawling around on hands and knees.

'So keep your eyes and ears open. Your father's watching you and he has important messages for you. But only Arkhad alone has the power to unlock the sacred door to the heavenly realms of spirits.'

She unclasped a fist, revealing a small golden envelope.

'This is a secret for you alone, Herbert,' she whispered. 'Do not mention it to anybody, especially your mother. And do not open it before the sixth evening hour. Otherwise, your secret will vanish from your sight.'

'Thanks Madame Mistral,' Herbert said, taking the small, golden envelope.

'Be strong, Herbert. Face your fears,' Madame Mistral continued. 'And your father's love will fill your heart, never to diminish.'

Herbert was just about to reply when his mum dragged him by the arm. 'Come on,' she hissed, her tongue sticking out like a venomous snake's. 'I've had enough of all this silly nonsense!'

'Get out of my tent, Suzanne Humphries,' Madame Mistral yelled. 'Stay here any longer and true love will always hide in the deepest, darkest caverns of your heart, *never* to be discovered.'

'Thanks for that,' Mum barked, flicking her fringe out of her eyes. 'Go and discover a proper job for yourself.'

As everybody strolled away, Madame Mistral howled like an injured puppy. 'Arkhad's bone has spoken,' she cried, rolling around on the damp grass. 'Your future fates are sealed, so BEWARE...'

She sprung up, locking her knobbly knees together. 'I'm wetting myself!' she yelled, throwing her arms around her waist. Hobbling away, she disappeared down a passageway, into another part of the tent.

'Oh that silly woman's put me in a right foul mood now!' Mum exclaimed, throwing her head into her hands as she walked. 'Oh forget about her,' Trevor said, squeezing her hand. 'She's just not worth it.'

Herbert piped up. 'Yes, but how on earth did she know our names?'

'She obviously heard us all talking when we walked into the tent, Herb,' Trevor said. 'Maybe she's got a hidden microphone or something?'

'Well I don't know,' Herbert muttered, feeling Madame Mistral's envelope, safely resting in his pocket. 'It all seems a bit, well, strange if you ask me.'

'Well it's all your fault, Trevor!' Mum snapped. 'I mean, we could have spent that money in the Arcade. What a waste!'

'I suppose you're right,' Trevor said, shaking his head. 'I was only doing it for you, Herb!'

'Well I still think there's something mysterious about her though and - '

'Oh Herbert,' his mum said, interrupting his flow. 'Let's forget all about Madame Mistral now and start to enjoy ourselves for a change!'

'Your mum's right, Herb,' Trevor said.

'I know,' Herbert replied, catching hold of his mum's other hand. 'But how did she know our names?'

'Herbert!' his mum yelled, banging the sole of her right boot hard onto the floor. 'I can feel this mood coming back! Any more talk about that silly woman and I'm going straight home – and I'll be taking you with me!'

Herbert sauntered on, strolling along with his mum and Trevor. But like locks without keys, unanswered questions about that strange old lady gyrated around Herbert's mind. And they wouldn't stop.

THIRTEEN

'Perfect!' Trevor exclaimed, marching towards the 'Hook a duck' stall.

He pushed to the front of the queue, pulling Herbert in with him. 'I'll pay for you Herb, if you want a go,' he said. 'I've always loved the 'Hook a duck' stall.'

'Oh, err, thanks Trevor,' Herbert replied, forcing out a smile. 'But I'm ok thanks.'

'Never mind ok,' Trevor said, grinding his teeth. 'Come on. Let's have a go – together!'

Squeezing into tiny gaps in the crowd, Herbert and Trevor waited around. A pretty teenage assistant handed them two bamboo fishing rods. Magnetic hooks dangled from their ends, attached to long, nylon strings. The yellow ducks bounced around on the calm, circling water, minding their own business.

Herbert's luck was in. 'Got one!' he cried, drawing his rod out of the water. The assistant turned the duck over. 'No number, no winner,' she said. 'Better luck next time!'

Herbert crumpled up his face. 'Just my luck,' he said. 'I never win anything.'

'That'll do me!' Trevor shouted as he managed to hook up a fleeing duck. The same assistant unhooked the trapped, plastic bird. 'I hope he's not in pain,' Trevor chuckled, handing in his fishing rod.

'Brian,' the assistant said, reading out the small black letters on the duck's belly. 'You've won a blow up banana. Congratulations!'

'Hold on a minute, Trevor,' Herbert said, scratching his wiry hair. 'That's the duck's name that Madame Mistral mentioned. And didn't she say something about holding onto a banana?'

'I think she did, Herb,' Trevor said, clutching his enormous prize. 'I'll have to be careful!'

Herbert and Trevor walked back to Mum. The tale blurted from their lips.

'You two will believe anything,' she said. 'And anyway, what's dangerous about a blow up banana?'

'You never know,' Trevor chuckled. 'If I get attacked by a hungry gorilla, it could be curtains!'

Herbert tried to stop it but he couldn't. His ribs vibrated, tickled by a loud, unexpected guffaw. His mum joined in the chorus, laughing whilst shaking her head.

That was hilarious, Herbert thought. He stared at Trevor. He was pretending to eat his banana, slurping like a hungry horse. Then he turned around. 'Has anybody got any custard?' he asked, munching on his prize's yellow plastic. 'I'm starving!'

Once more, a giggle flew out of Herbert's mouth.

'See, he's not all that bad, is he?' Mum whispered to her son, squeezing his hand. 'So just give him a break, eh?'

Still thinking about Madame Mistral's number thirteen, Herbert remained quiet. Then, the grating, distorted sounds of an ice-cream van's music barged into his ears, blasting out of two large speakers.

'Anybody fancy a '99'?' Trevor asked, striding up to the van's serving hatch. 'Oh yes please,' Herbert and his mum chorused.

A short, bald headed man appeared. A small pair of gold-rimmed spectacles rested upon his nose. 'Three 99's please!' Trevor exclaimed, parking his enormous elbows on the counter. 'With lashings of raspberry!'

'No problem, mate,' the man replied, pulling three naked cornets out of a box.

Mum grabbed at her flake, popping it into her mouth. She wrapped her tongue around a smooth ball of ice cream, licking it heartily. Then she screamed out a powerful shout, dropping her cornet onto the grass.

Passers-by stopped to look as she jumped around in the air, riding an invisible pogo stick. She opened up her mouth. Blood poured off her tongue, dripping off her chin. Bending down, she picked up the remains of her cornet, covered in dust and dirt. She plunged her fingers into the cold, thick mixture, pulling something out.

'I don't believe it,' she bawled; holding up a long, silver screw. 'What on earth's going on?'

FOURTEEN

Marching over to the ice-cream van, Mum threw her cornet at the grass. She banged her fists hard on the van's metal side. The ice cream man popped his head out of his hatch, fixing his spectacles. Mum held up the dangerous object, still coated in the melting, milky mixture.

'Your ice cream's dangerous!' she yelled, waving the screw around.

'It's not my fault,' the man snapped. 'I only buy the stuff, I don't make it!'

The ice cream man shut his hatch with a bang. He flicked a small lock on the side, before sliding into the driver's seat. Then he turned his 'ice-cream' music up, to its highest, ear splitting volume. Pulling a newspaper out, he buried his head in it, ignoring Mum's hard banging.

Hobbling along, an old lady stopped to look, balancing on a walking stick. A long, black coat hung from her thin body, almost touching the floor. Black wellington boots, covered in dried mud, stuck out at the bottom. Thick, fur gloves hid her hands. A green, velvet hat covered her wispy grey hair. Her eyes, magnified by enormous black spectacles, burned bright, like locomotive lamps in a tunnel.

'Turn that blasted music down, will you?' she screamed, shooting a fearsome, fiery stare at Mum. 'It's driving me mad! My hearing aid's buzzing!'

She dropped her walking stick onto the muddy turf. Then she lost her balance and collapsed into a heap. 'Don't you worry,' Trevor yelled, dashing over. 'I've got my Boy Scouts' 'helping old people' badge – first class!'

But as Trevor was pulling her to her feet, disaster struck. The old lady's hearing aid overheated. Thick, black smoke poured out of it, rising up into the sky. The electronic hearing aid exploded into a thousand pieces, accompanied by a loud bang.

The old lady's right ear split open and a mixture of plastic, blood and electronic wires shot through the air.

'My ear!' the old lady cried, displaying her false teeth like a wild dog. She picked up her walking stick, pointing it at Herbert. 'You've broken my hearing aid, haven't you?' she screamed. 'I'll have you for that!'

'I don't know what you're talking about,' Herbert shouted.

'You know what you've done!' the old lady shouted back.

'He hasn't done anything!' Mum barked, barging past the old lady.

Everybody trotted away, disappearing into the crowd. 'Who on earth was that?' Trevor asked, stretching his jaw.

'I don't know,' Mum replied. 'But whoever she was, I'm certainly glad she's gone!'

'She was mad!' Herbert chuckled. 'Stark, raving mad!'

***

Herbert, his mum and Trevor headed towards a refreshment tent. 'Oh let's have a drink at last,' Trevor said, joining the queue. 'I'm gasping!'

In the distance, a high-pitched shouting match shook the ground. A teenage boy was arguing with his sister, pushing into her with his palms.

Stepping out of the queue, Mum stopped to look. The boy stuffed a long piece of aniseed rock into his mouth. Screaming at his little sister, he spat out tiny pieces of candy.

'Rock's good for your teeth,' he shouted.

'No it's not!'

'Yes it is!'

The sister sprinted away. The boy's face burned red. He removed the huge lump of rock from his mouth. Aiming it at his sister's head, he flung it through the air like a warrior throwing a dagger.

It missed its target but plunged straight into Mum's face. Dancing stars gathered, clouding her vision. Stumbling back, she didn't notice a huge, overweight man, his body as wide as a Highland cow.

Standing on a small red and silver box, he was wearing an old fashioned black suit, his bulging belly bursting out of its white shirt. A tall top hat sat on the top of his fat head, held in place by a tight leather strap, hooked underneath one of his chins.

'Balloons, balloons!' his strong voice bellowed out. 'Two balloons for a fiver!'

He was clutching two handfuls of enormous red balloons, thirty-five in number. They floated high above him on their long strings. But as Mum stumbled into him, the balloon seller lost his balance. He tumbled off his pedestal, crashing into the ground. His head plunged into a large rock, knocking him out.

Yearning for freedom, the balloons reached for the sky, their smooth strings sliding through the man's chubby fingers. Mum dived through the air, aiming her hands at the escaping strings. 'I'll save them for you!' she shouted, grabbing at their strings.

Pulling several balloons towards her, Mum stretched out her body. She sprung up into the air, catching a few more. But as she got hold of another group of balloons, the soles of her shoes lifted up, clean off the ground. And eager to escape as fast as possible, the helium balloons hauled Mum up into the sky.

'Somebody help!' she cried, floating higher and higher. She tried to release the strings. But somehow, invisible super-glue held them in place.

Herbert and Trevor sprinted over. They both catapulted into the air, hoping to grab Mum's long legs. But it was no good. She was out of everybody's reach. Soon, she was a distant blob of red, high up in the sky.

The fairground manager dashed over to Herbert and Trevor, his colourful tie bouncing around in the wind. 'I'll inform the police as soon as possible,' he remarked. 'Oh and don't worry, somebody will eventually pick her up.'

'I just hope it's not from the floor,' Trevor sobbed, wiping his eyes.

'I'm just going to call air traffic control on the emergency telephone,' the manager announced. 'But I'm sure she'll land safely.'

The manager sprinted away into the distance, parting the gathering crowd. Herbert screamed out loud, like an injured piglet. Thick tears tumbled down his cheeks. 'I don't want mum to die, Trevor,' he squealed.

'Madame Mistral's right, Herb,' Trevor whimpered. 'Everything's coming true and your mum was laughing at her and - '

'She shouldn't have tried to steal Arkhad's bone,' Herbert cried, rubbing his eyes with sweaty hand.

'Oh don't worry, Herb,' Trevor sniffled. 'I'm sure she'll be all right. And anyway, your mum didn't steal the bone in the end, did she?'

'Yes but what if - '

'Well that Madame Mistral woman might be a bit of a weirdo,' Trevor interrupted. 'But I don't think she'd kill anybody.'

'Yes, but everything she said seems to be coming true, Trevor,' Herbert said, clicking his knuckles one after the other.

'I know, Herb,' Trevor answered, placing his huge hands onto Herbert's shoulders. 'This day's turning into a right old disaster.'

Trevor rubbed Herbert's cheeks, smoothing his red, tear soaked face with two chunky thumbs. 'But hey, don't you worry, Herb,' he mumbled in a low but strong voice. 'I'm sure your mum'll land safely; fingers crossed eh?'

'Yes, but whatever's next Trevor?' Herbert stammered, kicking a stone across the grass.

'I dread to think,' Trevor replied.

106

FIFTEEN

'Come on, Herb,' Trevor announced, zipping up his jacket. 'I'm going home. There's no way I'm staying around here after what's happened to your mum.'

'But we can't go home yet, Trevor,' Herbert replied. 'Don't you remember what Madame Mistral said? All that about the fifth hour?'

'Oh I wouldn't believe in all that mumbo jumbo, Herb,' Trevor chuckled, his lips spreading into half a smile. 'We just need to find your poor mum, that's all.'

'I don't think it's worth taking the risk, Trevor,' Herbert said, staring through Trevor's damp, enlarging eyes.

'Well I remember her saying something about not leaving until five o'clock,' Trevor muttered. 'But there's no way I'm staying here when your mum's up in that sky, Herbert!'

Trevor sucked in and puffed out a pocket of air. Closing his eyes, he dropped his head. He collapsed onto a wide, wooden bench, his thick body sinking into the wood. 'Because if anything's happened to Suzanne, I don't know what I'll do.'

Herbert parked his body next to Trevor's. *I love you Dad,* he thought. He peered up into the wide, blue sky. An enormous cloud was drifting by, its white, fluffy mass stretching out across the great expanse. *So can you keep Mum safe, please? I don't want her to die.*

Two lonely tears dropped out of Herbert's eyes, cascading down his cheeks. 'It's all my fault really,' he stuttered, leaning against Trevor. 'It was all my idea to go into Madame Mistral's tent.'

'Don't blame yourself, Herb,' Trevor whimpered. 'I didn't want to go in at all, really. And I only said yes because I was trying to make you happy. It's been very difficult recently and - '

Trevor's sentence was cut off. Gasping for breath, the fairground manager galloped up to the bench. His shoes screeched to a halt in front of Trevor, sending up a cloud of earthy dust.

'Oh at last,' he said, hauling in gulps of oxygen. 'I've been looking for you two all over the place.'

He turned towards Trevor, sucking in another lungful of precious air. 'Your wife's fine Sir!' he exclaimed, thrusting his hands onto his hips.

'It's all a bit mad really but to cut a long story short, a flock of seagulls attacked the balloons and most of them popped! So your wife just floated down, sort of like an invisible parachute was strapped to her back. It's a miracle if you ask me.'

'Wow, so where did she land?' Trevor asked. 'Is she injured?'

'Well she managed to land on a giant trampoline in somebody's back garden,' the manager replied. 'On top of twin girls, I heard! But as far as I know, nobody was seriously injured.'

'Oh that's great!' Trevor exclaimed, springing up to shake the manager's hand. 'Thanks for all your help!'

'Your wife's in Newton hospital, so don't you worry about a thing!' the manager continued. 'Everything's turned out fine! Somebody up there's looking after her, that's for sure!'

'Brilliant news!' Herbert cried, waving a tight, clenched fist through the air as he looked up into the sky. 'Thanks Dad!'

'Anyway, great news and enjoy the rest of your day,' the manager said, dashing away.

'There you go, Herb,' Trevor shouted, throwing a long arm around Herbert's shoulder. 'Your mum's fine! So that's great, isn't it? Your dad's looking after her and I'll tell you that for nothing!'

'I know,' Herbert beamed, raising his eyes to the heavens.

'Anyway, let's go for some fish and chips,' Trevor announced. 'I'm famished!'

'Sounds great,' Herbert chuckled, puffing out his cheeks as his lips exploded into a giggle. 'What's so funny?' Trevor asked.

'Well that manager thinks my mum's your wife!' Herbert explained, trying to stifle his giggle.

'Oh I know, everybody presumes that, all the time,' Trevor replied, wrapping his other arm around Herbert's head and squeezing him like a friendly wrestler. 'Happens a lot! Anyway, I'm on the top of world now! Suzanne's alive and well and fish and chips is next! I'm as happy as a pig in muck!'

Like lost, somersaulting coins in a washing machine, Madame Mistral's magical, mysterious words tumbled around Herbert's mind. 'Trevor,' he asked. 'Do you think we should go home now or wait until after five?'

'Well I've been thinking about that, Herb,' Trevor replied, unwrapping his arms from Herbert's head. 'And I think you're right. After what's happened to your mum, I don't think we can chance it.'

'Well at least we know Mum's fine,' Herbert said. 'So we might as well hang around until five o'clock anyway.'

'Then we can go straight to the hospital on the way home,' Trevor said.

'Yes, that's a great idea,' Herbert answered, nodding his head.

'Anyway, if we did leave before five o'clock and things turned nasty,' Trevor added, 'we'd never forgive ourselves!'

'You're right, Trevor,' Herbert replied.

'Well there you go then,' Trevor exclaimed, his lips arching into a grin at long last. 'Come on; let's enjoy ourselves, Herb. If your mum's alright, we're alright!'

'So fish and chips it is then!' Herbert shouted, dancing off with Trevor at his side.

SIXTEEN

Herbert and Trevor strolled around the fairground, eyeing up all the different shows, stalls and rides. 'Wow, look at that!' Herbert yelled, peering through his glasses. He jumped up and down, his boots squashing the grass beneath him.

Herbert pointed at a giant roller coaster. Perched on the top of tall girders, the roller coaster's high, bending tracks almost touched low flying clouds. A deafening 'whoosh' sound burst out over their heads as a long train of cars thundered along.

'Why don't you have a go, Herb?' Trevor asked, staring up at the marvellous, metallic monster. 'Err, no, I'll give it a go next time,' Herbert said, avoiding Trevor's eyes. 'I've got a headache and my stomach feels all tight. But why don't you have a go? You love rollercoasters; I remember you telling me.'

'Err, well, it's getting late and to be honest I'm a bit thirsty,' Trevor replied, his face deepening into a scarlet red colour. 'So why don't we just go for a drink?'

'Well Jack in school reckons his dad's been on the largest roller coaster in the world,' Herbert announced. 'Somewhere in Florida, I think.'

'Oh,' Trevor said, kicking at a clump of grass.

'Oh come on Trevor, I thought you said you *loved* rollercoasters!' Herbert exclaimed.

'Well I suppose we'd better find out how your mum's getting on,' Trevor said, his voice hardly a whisper. He pulled his mobile phone from his pocket and pressed several digits. Soon, he was chatting away to a nurse.

'Your mum's fine, Herb,' he said, pressing the end call button. 'She's comfortable and asleep at the moment.'

'Ah, that's great,' Herbert replied. 'I knew she'd be ok, somehow. But we still have to hang around until five, remember. So why not have a go of that roller coaster?'

'Err, well, it's just that - '

'Go on Trevor!' Herbert added. 'Show me how brave you are!'

Walking on ahead, Trevor kicked a little dust from his shoes, lowering his head. 'It's getting late as well, Herb,' he added. 'And I'm thirsty and my legs are hurting and - '

'Oh come on, Trevor,' Herbert interrupted, sticking his hands deep into his pockets. 'If Jack's dad can do it, I'm sure you can.'

He stared at Trevor, switching on a strong 'Do it for me!' look. 'We'd all be so proud of you, especially Mum,' he added.

Craning his head up, Trevor glanced up at the train of cars. They whooshed past overhead, their wheels skidding along the high, twisting tracks. Trevor's heart slipped into 'emergency' beating mode. Beads of sweat squeezed out of the pores on his forehead. He coughed out a loud pocket of air, tapping his right foot up and down.

Well I'll definitely impress Herb if I do it, Trevor thought, running his palm over his scalp. 'Oh go on then,' he stuttered. 'Just for you, Herb.'

'Mum'll be so proud of you,' Herbert exclaimed, arching his eyebrows.

Herbert and Trevor sauntered towards the roller coaster's entrance. 'At least the queue's not very big,' Herbert said. He pointed to a short line of people, hanging around on a steep flight of metal steps. 'Anyway, I'll wait here, Trevor,' Herbert said. 'Don't forget to wave to me when you're up there!'

'I'll try,' Trevor said, nodding his head. 'Sure you don't want to join me?'

'Err, no,' Herbert replied. 'This headache's getting worse.'

'Ok,' Trevor said, grabbing the steps' handrail. 'See you in a mo.'

Trevor climbed up, one step at a time. The queue weaved its way towards the front of the ride. Looking at a large sign, lit up by bright, neon lights, Trevor's eyes enlarged. Every muscle in his thick body trembled, creating a cold, spine tingling shiver.

'The 'Demon Dragon' the flickering neon sign said. 'Probably the fastest ride in the world!'

What on earth am I doing up here? Trevor thought, pressing into the barrier at the top of the steps. He peered at Herbert, standing below. *I suppose Herb won't think I'm a wimp if I have a go. And he might even start to like me for a change...*

An attendant pulled up the barrier. Trevor walked along the long train of stationary cars. *I must be stark raving mad*, he thought as he squashed his big body into his chosen car.

'Can you leave your banana here please?' the attendant asked. 'You can collect it at the end if you want to.'

'I'm sorry, mate,' Trevor answered, squeezing his giant prize into the car's cramped space. 'It's a long story but I can't let go of it today.'

'Well I suppose it can't do you any harm,' the attendant replied, shrugging his shoulders.

The attendant strolled towards the control booth. Of course, Trevor didn't notice the number painted on the side of his car. It was the number thirteen, its digits painted onto the car's bright red sides in glossy white paint.

Madame Mistral's words tormented Herbert. They danced around his mind like hot sparks streaming from a firework. A silent, strange feeling brushed his bones. Then a wild thought pierced his brain...

Hey, what's the number on Trevor's car? he thought, craning his neck as he looked at the roller coaster's long train of cars. The platform was almost as high as an electricity pylon.

Positioned in front of Trevor's car, a criss-cross lattice of iron girders obscured its numbers.

Oh that's fine, Herbert thought, his eyes digesting the distant digits. *Number thirty-one should be safe.*

SEVENTEEN

The Demon dragon's giant engine clicked into gear. Enormous metal cogs, coated in oil, turned and crunched, pushing a long line of cars along.

'I'm just going to the toilet,' Herbert shouted up to Trevor. But being too high up, Trevor couldn't hear a word. The 'Demon dragon' started its slow ascent. A long, metal chain clinked and clanked, pulling the train of cars up a steep incline. Trevor's face was as grey as a thundercloud. He grabbed the safety bar in front of him, wrapping his white fingers around its cold steel.

Sprinting towards the toilet block, Herbert tripped over, grazing his knee. 'Stupid laces,' he snapped, loosely tying the ends together. 'They're always coming undone.'

His hands shaking, Trevor attempted to tighten his loose safety belt over his protruding belly. He struggled to stretch the belt over his blow up banana prize. Then, disaster struck. He yanked the old, worn belt upwards. Two worn, rusty screws catapulted into the air. The frayed, leather belt broke loose from its fixings on the left side of the car.

'Somebody help!' Trevor yelled, clutching a length of limp leather. 'My belt's broken!'

At last, the Demon Dragon reached the top of its steep hill. The dragging chain clanked to an abrupt halt. The Dragon's cars balanced on the edge of the hill's summit. Then they plunged downhill. The train of cars raced at great speed along their rickety tracks.

Everybody let out high, cloud-bursting shouts, squeals and screams, filling the air with laughter. Trevor clung to the car's sides, his blood filled heart almost exploding. 'Stop the ride!' he roared as the Dragon flew around a corner on two wheels.

Nobody heard his cries for help. Flinging their arms up into the air, everybody scrunched up their faces into freeze frames of fabulous fun. The 'Dragon' shot around another sharp bend. The wind battered Trevor's body, stretching his face. Trevor clung to the sides of the car, clamping his eyes shut.

'I'm going to die!' he shrieked as the Dragon approached its most notorious part - the UPSIDE DOWN BIT! The Dragon twisted around, changing course in mid-air. Trevor's car hurtled around a hairpin bend, its little wheels almost leaving the tracks.

Then the inevitable happened. The train of cars turned upside down, thundering around another tight bend. Momentum alone held the train's wheels in place. Everybody laughed and cheered, 'saved' by tight safety belts. Except one man, hanging onto the sides of car number thirteen.

Trevor tipped out of the car. He plunged towards the ground, still hanging onto his big banana. His body tumbled and twisted through the air, in a fast, furious, free-fall spin.

'Help!' he screamed, his eyes, like huge gobstoppers, bulging out of their sockets.

But 'Lady Luck' was on his side. He landed with a bang, in the back seat of the swinging pirate ship. His giant, blow up banana cushioned his fall. His head jerked backwards, knocking him out cold.

Trevor drifted off, into a deep slumber, snoring like a snoozing hippopotamus. But the force of his powerful landing jammed the pirate ship's engine's gears. Nobody could stop its swishing, swinging, up and down movements.

EIGHTEEN

Herbert's feet ground to a sudden halt. The 'Valdorama', the fairground's big wheel, stood before him. Its sights and sounds mesmerized him, reeling him in.

So this is what Madame Mistral was talking about? he thought. He stared up at its enormous structure, towering higher and higher into the sky like a metallic spider's web. It spun around gently, accompanied by a jolly pipe organ waltz.

An enormous sign hung above the control booth:

Are you afraid of heights OR are you afraid of the Valdorama?

'Wow, it's amazing!' Herbert whispered, stretching up his neck. He gazed at the wheel's long lines of bright, multi-coloured bulbs, flashing on and off in sequence.

As the 'Valdorama' rotated around, Madame Mistral's unforgettable words entered his brain. *But first, you must conquer your fear of heights, my friend!*

Hypnotised by the Valdorama's dancing lights and music, Herbert stepped forwards. But a cast iron thought, looming over his head, penetrated his mind. *It's far too high for me. And anyway, what if I fall out?* That invisible thought chomped away at his brain cells, digging a hole.

Herbert walked away. He kicked a discarded drinks can across the grass. But then, he turned around. He locked his eyes onto the Valdorama's huge, steel structure. It cut into the air, lighting up the sky with its streaming, multi-coloured lights.

Well I suppose Trevor will buy me those trainers if I have a go, he thought. His eyes spun around as his gaze followed the enormous, rotating wheel. Once again, he strolled towards the Valdorama, pushing his way through a small crowd to get a closer look.

'Are you having a go, or what?' an old, almost bald attendant asked, his wispy grey hair dancing around on the top of his head. 'You've been hanging around here for ever, son!'

'Err, I'm just thinking about it,' Herbert muttered, folding his arms.

'Well you'd better hurry up,' the attendant chortled. 'It'll be closing time before you make your mind up!'

'Is it safe?'

Shaking his thin head, the attendant laughed. 'Val's over a hundred years old, son,' he remarked. 'And as far as I know, there's never been any problems in all that time, so I doubt if she's going to start now!'

He looked straight through Herbert, his old eyes sparkling like stars in the night-sky. 'They say Queen Victoria herself rode the Valdorama, way back in 1850. So if it's good enough for royalty, I'm sure it's good enough for you!'

A sudden puff of invisible white smoke exploded over Herbert's head. Madame Mistral's wise words taunted his muddled mind. *Face your fears, my friend!*

The man beckoned Herbert forwards, stepping down a few steps. He shouted out Madame Mistral's phrase, almost word for word. 'What are you waiting for? Come on - face your fears!'

A cold, ghostly shiver shook every cell of Herbert's body.

'Err, well, oh go on then,' he said, stepping onto a small set of steps. 'It's now or never.'

'Good show,' the man exclaimed. 'You won't regret it; it's a once in a lifetime experience!'

The attendant lifted up the barrier. Herbert walked across a wide, metal platform, sliding his hand across a safety rail. Then he pulled open a little door, climbing into a basket.

He spun his head around, looking for Trevor. But of course, he couldn't see him anywhere.

I bet he's having another go of the Dragon, Herbert thought. *I knew he'd love it.*

Herbert closed the basket's door and the attendant fixed a metal safety bar across his thighs.

'Who's this?' Herbert asked, pointing to a body, slumped on the wooden slatted seat beside him. A thick pink blanket covered the motionless body, like an old, forgotten curtain.

'Oh take no notice of old Mrs Hunter,' the attendant said, raising a chuckle. 'She comes every day at the same time and just falls asleep! And she always puts that daft blanket over her head.'

'Oh right,' Herbert said, sliding his bottom across the smooth, wooden seat.

'Don't worry, the old bat won't wake up!' the attendant shouted, trotting off towards the control booth. The motors cranked into gear.

Herbert tapped his feet, stopping a sharp attack of pins and needles. He closed his eyes, sucking up a deep breath of air. His ribs expanded as he curled his fingers tight around the safety bar.

'Are you ready to ride the Valdorama?' the attendant screamed, pouring his words into a powerful P.A. system. 'Because HERE WE GO!'

NINETEEN

The Valdorama started its rotating journey. A jolly waltz blasted through organ pipes, mixed with people's laughter. The gigantic wheel cut through the air with a gentle whooshing sound, building up speed. Hundreds of multi-coloured light bulbs formed a bright, circular stream, like an enormous Catherine wheel.

It's not all that bad, Herbert thought, his fingers curling around the metal safety bar.

'Do you wanna go faster?' the attendant's voice announced, screaming through the loudspeakers. 'Yeah!' the passengers screamed back.

A soft, muffled voice sound weaved its way into Herbert's ears. It seemed to be coming from under the pink blanket. 'Where am I? Am I camping?'

Herbert turned his head, observing the blanket.

An invisible hand punched at the pink, fluffy material, trying to escape. Herbert couldn't help it. His giggle valve vibrated and an enormous laugh burst through his lips.

A glove-covered hand appeared, tugging at the blanket. The hand pulled the blanket away, tossing it over the side of the basket.

An old aged pensioner gawped at Herbert, throwing out a razor sharp stare. 'What the devil are you doing here?' she snarled, squashing up her eyes.

Oh no, Herbert thought, recognising the old lady.

'I know you, don't I?' she snapped. 'You're the boy who stole my walking stick!'

'I didn't steal anything!' Herbert barked.

'Now where is it?'

'Who knows?' Herbert said, turning his gaze towards a distant aeroplane. 'You're mad, so just leave me alone!'

'You murdered Tommy, didn't you?' Mrs Hunter hissed, squaring up to Herbert's face.

Stretching out her long neck, Mrs Hunter gazed over the side of the basket. The skin on her ghostly grey face stretched. Her eyes almost dropped out of their small, wrinkly sockets. She gripped the sides of the Valdorama's basket, scrunching up her face like a dried out sponge.

'What the devil am I doing up here?' she roared, covering her eyes. 'I'm terrified of heights, ever since I fell off Blackpool tower years ago! I was pushed, actually, but nobody believes me. A clown from the circus – '

'Yes, whatever,' Herbert interrupted, cutting off her story.

Mrs Hunter pulled off her two black, velvet gloves, throwing them over the side. The gloves flipped up into the air before plunging towards the ground. 'Now look what you've done!' she screamed, shooting another sharp stare at Herbert. 'You've lost my gloves.'

'Yes, whatever,' Herbert said, sliding his body across the small, wooden seat.

Seizing Herbert's arm, Mrs Hunter squeezed into his body. 'You'll save me, won't you?' she asked. 'Even if you are a walking stick robber.'

Herbert pulled away. Clutching the steel safety bar, he looked into the whites of Mrs Hunter's eyes. 'I've told you,' he barked, snapping out his words using a slow, sharp delivery. 'I DIDN'T STEAL YOUR STICK!'

'Sick?' Mrs Hunter cried, throwing her head into her hands. 'You're going to be sick?'

Grasping its metal sides, Mrs Hunter started to rock the basket to and fro. 'And I'm wearing my new, pure wool coat!' she cried. 'Stop the ride! Vomit alert, vomit alert!'

'I didn't say that!' Herbert barked, banging the safety bar with two flat palms. 'I'm not going to be sick, so do me a favour and just shut up!'

Mrs Hunter attempted to stand up in the little basket. The safety bar stopped her, so she dropped her body into her seat. The Valdorama continued to spin around in the air like a gigantic hamster's wheel.

Mrs Hunter thrust her head over the basket's side once more. 'Help!' she yelled, shaking her head around. 'This thug's going to be sick all over my new coat! He's got no respect!'

'Shut up, you old witch!' Herbert screamed, curling up fingers and toes.

Mrs Hunter twisted her eyes around, scanning the ground below. Her green hat fell off her head. It drifted through the air towards the ground. A hungry seagull swooped low. It clamped the hat in its beak, flying away with its prize.

'Arrest that seagull!' Mrs Hunter screamed, banging the basket's sides. 'It's stolen my hat!'

Mrs Hunter fixed her long, grey hair, blowing in the breeze like broken spiders' webs.

135

She brushed a bony hand over her thinning grey locks. Then she snarled at Herbert, staring at him with fiery eyes. 'You've stolen my hat, haven't you?' she yelled.

Herbert couldn't stop himself. 'It was the seagull, you fool,' he said. His chuckle muscles rolled up and down and he giggled. 'Nobody laughs at me and gets away with it!' Mrs Hunter shrieked, attempting to stand up.

She dragged in a long, deep breath, her cheeks sucking inwards. Like a circus contortionist, Mrs Hunter managed to squeeze her thin waist and thighs under the safety bar. Soon, she was standing upright on the basket's wooden seat, hanging onto a girder.

'Can the person in the blue basket sit down please?' the operator's voice asked.

'Nobody tells me to sit down and gets away with it!' Mrs Hunter cried.

Still standing, Mrs Hunter rocked the basket to and fro, holding onto its metal sides.

'Could you *please* sit down?' the operator's voice shouted out again. 'Or I'll have to stop the ride.'

'Sit down you old bag!' Herbert screamed, gripping the safety bar. 'You're going to kill us!'

The operator pressed the Valdorama's emergency stop button. The giant motor's electricity supply shut off. The Valdorama slowed down, its hundreds of multi coloured bulbs still blazing bright. Soon, the enormous wheel ground to a halt. Herbert's basket stopped in the cold air, at the wheel's highest possible point.

Mrs Hunter popped out her eyes, snarling at Herbert like a hungry pit bull terrier. 'You stole my walking stick *and* my hat!' she yelled. 'You'll be stealing my knickers next, so this is your punishment!'

Balancing like a windsurfer, Mrs Hunter increased her strength, rocking the basket even further. 'Please sit down!' the operator's voice bellowed from below.

Herbert filled his lungs with air. He sucked and sucked, dragging in oxygen. Squeezing his waist and thighs through the safety bar, he stood up straight. He pushed into his foe with two flat palms but his efforts had no effect.

'Do you know I'm a yellow belt in karate?' Mrs Hunter belched. She raised her arm, landing a karate style chop onto Herbert's shoulders.

Herbert cried out, scrunching up his face. His legs buckled and he tumbled over. Struggling to get up, he glanced over the basket's thick, metal rim. *Look how high up you are, Herbert?* a voice grated, bouncing around his mind. *You're going to fall out. But can you beat your fears?*

A sudden surge of sickness invaded Herbert's body. He tried to pull himself up but couldn't. His fear of heights grabbed onto his ankles like invisible hands, rooting him to the spot.

Rocking the basket ever faster, Mrs Hunter stood strong. Her wellington boots seemed to be screwed to the basket's floor. Herbert's bent up body lay motionless on the seat. Tiny stars darted around his eyes. A cloud of dizziness swept over his head.

'Nobody messes with Hilary Hunter and gets away with it!' the old lady cried. She rocked the basket faster and faster, sending it closer and closer towards its tipping point.

That strange, ghostly voice whispered another message, tormenting Herbert's mind. *Of course you're going to be world famous, aren't you? You'll be the boy who fell off the Valdorama. And died. That's what's going to happen if you don't stand up and fight!*

An incredible surge of electrical energy raced through Herbert's veins. He pulled his body up, wrenching his spine from his seat. Soon he was standing head to head with his enemy. He peered into Mrs Hunter's eyes, like a boxer before a big fight.

'And *nobody* messes with Herbert Humphries!' he yelled. 'And gets away with it!'

Herbert pushed into Mrs Hunter's body, punching her in the ribs. Her head tossed backwards. One of her old knees cracked with a click. Two sets of false teeth popped out of her jaws, flying through to the air. Gravity gripped them, pulling them towards the ground.

'You idiot!' Mrs Hunter screamed in a dull, muffled voice. 'Nobody will fancy me now! So prepare to meet thy maker!'

TWENTY

Mrs Hunter waved her arms around, twisting and turning. Her hands sliced through the air as she practised a sequence of judo moves.

'Hiya!' she yelled as thick veins popped out of her neck. Her right hand chopped into Herbert's head with a strong, deadly blow. She despatched another blow, ploughing into Herbert's shoulder with great force.

Herbert lost his footing. Once more, one of his long shoelaces trailed the basket's floor. He tripped up on it, stumbling backwards. His whole body almost tumbled out of the basket. He screamed out a war cry, saving himself by gripping onto a chrome door handle.

'I'll have you, you thief,' Mrs Hunter cried, kicking her boot into Herbert's body.

'I didn't steal anything!' Herbert spluttered, clutching his sides. He panted for precious breath. A great wash of tears invaded his eyes.

'Hiya!' Mrs Hunter yelled once more, karate chopping another hard, heavy blow towards her victim's head. But this time, Herbert was too quick for her.

He flicked his head to one side, dodging out of the way. Mrs Hunter's hand came crashing down onto the basket's steel rim. She cried out like a hungry hound, clutching her throbbing hand.

Blood gushed out of a large cut, dropping onto her coat. She clasped her other hand around her bloody injury and stared hard at Herbert.

'There's blood on my coat, now,' she screamed, moving in for the kill. 'Hiya!' she barked, chopping into Herbert with her other hand. But Herbert rolled out of her way. Mrs Hunter's hand collided with the back of the basket's wooden chair.

'Arrgghh!' she yelled, dragging her distorted hand up to her eyes.

Gathering below, a large crowd turned their heads towards the sky. They watched the scene unfold, launching eye stretching and jaw dropping gasps.

'I'll kill you if my knitting hand's broken!' Mrs Hunter shrieked. 'And I'm halfway through a scarf as well!'

Standing over her victim, like a dark, evil shadow, the old lady pulled at Herbert's coat, dragging him upwards. 'Help!' Herbert screamed, pushing her away. He jumped to his feet, holding his arms in front of his grey face.

'Hiya!' Mrs Hunter cried, cutting into Herbert's flesh. Herbert lost his balance. He tumbled over. Scrambling to his feet, he stood up on wobbly legs. 'Hiya!' his tormentor cried again, hacking into Herbert with a crack karate chop.

Again, Herbert was too fast for her. He grabbed Mrs Hunter's wrist, twisting it around. But she pulled up her other arm, aiming another lethal, chopping hand at Herbert's nose.

Herbert gripped this wrist too. Together they fought, barging into each other like two Sumo wrestlers. Until at last, it happened...

Sensing that old Mrs Hunter was losing her power, Herbert conjured up one final, gigantic thrust. He turned his power dial to 'Superhero' and supercharged his muscles. Stepping forwards, he pushed Mrs Hunter's body away with an enormous, super strength shove.

Herbert's arch-enemy's knees crashed into the basket's low wall of metal. Her legs buckled under her. Her body toppled over the basket's side. Armour piercing screams flew out of Mrs Hunter's mouth as her limp body plunged towards the ground. But sometimes, luck suddenly appears...

Mrs Hunter landed on the top of a passing trolley cage, pulled along by a fairground worker. A mountain of cuddly toy prizes was piled up in the cage and this cushioned her fall. She leapt down, rubbing her head before stumbling away into the crowd.

Herbert couldn't stop himself. Carried forwards by the momentum of his 'superhero' efforts, he imitated Mrs Hunter's exact movements. His shins smashed into the basket's low wall of steel. Tossing forwards, his body catapulted out. He closed his eyes, dropping into the unknown.

TWENTY ONE

For a change, the goddess of 'Good luck' befriended Herbert. One of his long, thick shoelaces tangled up in a tiny gap in between a nut and bolt. The lace had a large knot tied into the end of it. Sticking solid, it stopped Herbert's fall. The lace's thick, 'sports–scientific' fibres somehow took the strain of Herbert's bodyweight.

Our hero dangled in the air. His whole body hung upside down, suspended from his tight shoelace. *I don't want to die!* Herbert thought, glancing at a mass of people below him.

The growing crowd peered up into the sky. Locking their eyes onto the Valdorama's human bat, they thrust hands over gaping mouths. Screams of horror reached for the sky, almost splitting open a passing cloud.

Herbert's lace started to slide through the nut and bold. The lace slipped through the tiny gap, increasing its length by a centimetre. But an even bigger knot was further down the shoelace. It stopped as though God himself had commanded it to.

Herbert's heart slipped into 'danger' mode, beating like a thumping, subsonic bass. Every sinew in his body trembled. Hauling in two huge gulps of air, he closed his eyes. He waited for his drop into the unknown, wondering how much longer he had to live.

Word of the 'Boy bat' spread like a forest fire. A TV camera crew dashed to the scene. Their black helicopter landed on an open, grassy space, blowing up dust into everybody's faces.

Newspaper reporters arrived, hanging onto notebooks and tape recorders. They clicked away with their expensive cameras. They snapped hundreds of 'unbelievable' shots with lenses almost longer than drainpipes. Some people pulled mobiles from pockets, filming the memorable, heart-stopping scene.

***

'Hooray!' Trevor cried as technicians finally fixed the Pirate ship's overworked gearbox. The old wooden galleon swished to a halt. Everybody clambered down.

People staggered away like an army of drunkards. Their heads filled up with the sick, nauseating effects of dizziness. Others sprinted away to be sick. Trevor was lucky. He seemed to be fine.

Where on earth's Herb got to? Trevor thought, wandering around like a knight without a horse. His head twisted and turned full circle as he dashed across the dry, patchy grass. He sprinted through a maze of stalls, shows and rides.

'Herbert?' Trevor yelled, his trainers kicking up thick clouds of dust. 'Where are you, mate?'

Trevor marched past the 'Haunted mansion' ghost train. *Where's everybody gone?* he thought, glancing at a dozen, deserted carriages.

His head still spinning, he sprinted into a thick crowd of people, wading into the wall of flesh. They were all peering up into the sky, like hundreds of servants worshipping an ancient sun goddess.

What's happening here? Trevor thought. *I'll never find Herb in this crowd and believe me, if Herb's lost, Suzanne will kill me!*

'What's going on, mate?' Trevor shouted, tapping a man's shoulder.

'Somebody's stuck up there,' a stranger answered, pointing towards the sky. 'And I think he's hanging from one of his shoelaces.'

Trevor looked up, shading his eyes from the dying sunlight. His brain clicked into gear. He stretched his bones, standing on tiptoes. His eyes locked onto the figure dangling in the air. It resembled a spider, hanging around on a strong, silky thread.

A cold, tingling wind roared up the length of Trevor's spine, breaking the world speed shiver record. His lungs shut down, cutting off his air supply. Trevor's muscles froze up, his bones coated in a fine, frosty mist.

'Herbert!' he yelled, pushing his way through several walls of people, cemented together like bricks. 'Herbert!'

Reaching the front of the crowd, Trevor spotted the fairground manager. He was chatting to two policemen. Trevor sprinted over, barging into people and knocking them out of the way.

'What on earth's Herbert doing up there?' he snapped to the manager. 'There's been, well, some sort of accident and - '

'I'm sorry, Sir,' a tall policeman interrupted, clicking his boots. 'A fire engine will be here as soon as possible. But there's been an accident on the motorway, so it's been delayed.'

Sucking in a huge breath, Trevor pointed up with a long index finger. 'Well that boy's my girlfriend's son and if anything happens to him, I'll - '

'Don't worry, Sir, everything's under control,' the policeman's burly sidekick remarked, his hard voice grating into Trevor's face. 'The fire engine should be here in about half an hour and they've got extending ladders, so - '

'Half an hour?' Trevor barked, running a huge hand over his head. 'Are you joking? If that shoelace snaps, Herbert's got no chance!'

The policeman looked at Trevor, switching on his 'I know what I'm doing' voice.

'Look, Sir, there's been a very serious accident on the motorway. A huge pile up, with many casualties,' he snapped. Pointing at Herbert's dangling body, he turned towards Trevor.

'And it's obviously far too dangerous for anybody to try and climb up there, isn't it? And according to our 'Health and safety' regulations - '

'You can stuff your regulations,' Trevor cried out. 'I mean, that boy up there - '

As Trevor was talking, Herbert's shoelace dropped again, squeezing through the tiny gap in between the nut and bolt. The shoelace came to rest once more, another large knot saving Herbert's life. The crowd's ear piercing gasps and screams ascended into the air, hitting Herbert's ears.

TV camera crews rolled their cameras, shooting the scene. Satellites beamed it live into newsrooms across the world. Newspaper photographers clicked away, capturing Herbert's fate, second by second.

'Somebody help!' Herbert cried, closing his eyes. 'I don't want to die!'

'Right, that's it!' Trevor bellowed, sprinting towards the base of the Valdorama. The tall policeman chased after him, diving to trap Trevor's big thighs in a rugby tackle. He failed and landed in a muddy patch of grass. 'Don't do anything stupid, Sir,' the policeman shouted as

Trevor jumped onto the huge metal structure. 'A dead hero's no use to anybody.'

The tall policeman's radio crackled into life. 'The motorway's still closed,' a voice announced, breaking up on the airwaves. 'So a fire engine's on it's way from Ranleigh.'

'Ranleigh's miles away,' the policemen said to his sergeant, brushing down his uniform. Pointing at Trevor, the burly sergeant narrowed his eyes. 'I think that man might just be the boy's only chance.'

Herbert's eyes remained tight shut. His whole body trembled, causing his shoelace to shake. 'Somebody help me, please,' he whispered, his energy draining.

'Don't worry; Herb,' Trevor shouted from below, 'I'm coming up. I'll save you, mate!'

TWENTY TWO

Clambering up the metal structure, Trevor gripped the cold metal hard. He wrapped his arms around the Valdorama's metal girders, poking his feet into tight spaces in the metal structure. 'Almost there, Herb,' he panted, not looking down.

Trevor stretched his arm over the halfway point, gripping a steel bar. Down below, a loud, piercing siren wailed out a call. Trevor couldn't resist. He glanced down, losing his footing. Trevor's fear of heights gripped his throat, strangling his jugular vein.

'I can't go any further, Herb!' he screamed, shutting his eyes tight. 'Sorry mate.'

'Don't worry,' Herbert mumbled, his voice a faint whisper. 'You tried your best.'

Trevor's heart almost exploded. His wet and sticky palms slipped on the cold metal. His whole body trembled like a captured, treacherous traitor. Seconds melted into minutes. Unable to move, Trevor shook his head. 'I can't do it, Herb,' he mumbled. 'I'm too scared.'

'Try to move towards the side,' the police sergeant's voice shouted, speaking through a megaphone. 'The fire engine's on its way; it won't be long.'

Trevor still couldn't move. Fear tormented his mind, super-gluing him to the spot. But then he heard Herbert, wining and whimpering like a wild animal caught in a trap.

'Please help me, Trevor,' Herbert stuttered. 'I don't want to die…'

Trevor pulled open his eyes. Twisting his thick neck, he glanced up at Herbert.

'Don't worry; Herb,' he shouted out, 'I'll try again. I'll save you, mate!'

Madame Mistral's voice floated into Trevor's mind. Loud and clear, her words stood in front of his eyes, their letters cast out of stainless steel. *Just be yourself my friend. Follow your heart. And if you do, miracles will surround you, for the rest of your days.*

Trevor prized his body away from the steel girders. Streams of salty sweat poured out of his skin's pores, soaking his body. His heart switched into over-drive, pumping super-charged blood into his veins. 'Don't look down,' he chanted, gulping up oxygen.

'Go on, my friend,' Madame Mistral's voice whispered. 'You can do it, you know you can!'

Higher and higher Trevor climbed, refusing to look down. Gripping the Valdorama's long, steel arms, he hauled himself up. He puffed and panted, his muscles almost bursting. 'I'll save you, Herb,' he muttered. 'Don't you worry, mate!'

Trevor clambered up, close to Herbert's basket, crawling up to it like Spiderman. He pushed himself forwards with a huge rush of effort.

Soon, he was underneath Herbert's upside down head. Herbert, his face crimson, gasped for air. He looked across, straight into Trevor's big, damp eyes. 'Watch out Trevor,' he cried. 'Please be careful.'

As Trevor was stretching out an arm, the knot in Herbert's lace surrendered. Herbert's body jolted downwards. The remaining length of his lace slid through the tiny, life-saving space in between the nut and bolt. The crowd's gasps, screams and shrieks punched the air.

Herbert's body dropped down. 'Arrgghh!' he yelled, closing his eyes whilst clenching his fists. Trevor wedged his feet into two pockets between criss-crossing girders. He held out his other arm, catching Herbert's body and breaking his fall.

Trevor summoned up all his 'rugby training' strength. He pulled Herbert into his body, wrapping his arms around him. 'You're safe now, Herb,' he panted, holding Herbert in a headlock. Trevor twisted his right arm around, grabbing onto a steel girder. Shouts and cheers rose up out of the crowd. Clapping hands joined in with the chorus.

'Keep going Trevor,' Herbert wheezed. 'But don't look down whatever you do!'

Trevor's muscles almost ripped open as he struggled to move both himself and Herbert's body downwards. 'Don't look down, Trevor,' Herbert whispered. 'You're doing great!'

'That boy must be the luckiest boy in the world!' remarked a TV reporter, shouting into his microphone. 'A shoelace has saved this little boy's life, viewers! And this hero 'Spiderman' guy, whoever he is, seems to have appeared out of nowhere!'

At long last, a fire engine pushed its way through the crowd, its blue lights flashing. Fire fighters jumped out, sprinting away into different directions. As they prepared the ladders, Trevor stopped to rest. 'Oh thank God, Herb,' he panted. 'I thought I was gonna lose you.'

'Thanks Trevor,' Herbert replied, looking into Trevor with red, tear filled eyes. 'Thanks, well, you know, for saving my life and stuff and for being mum's boyfriend too, because - '

'I have two boys of my own,' Trevor said, interrupting Herbert's flow. 'Jamie and Lewis they're called. I just thought I'd tell you now, err, just in case I fall and don't make it. It's a long story but I lost my boys a few years ago, so that's why, well, err, that's why I'm not losing you too.'

Huge tears, like glass marbles, rolled out of Trevor's eyes.

'Jo and I split up you see and it wasn't very pleasant. She found somebody else and moved down to the south coast. And she took my two boys with her. I only see them once every blue moon. So perhaps you can understand now why I - '

An ear splitting, ghoulish scream exploded down below, sending shockwaves through the crowd. Still half way up the Valdorama, Trevor couldn't help it. He looked down.

An old lady was screaming and shouting, pushing through the wall of people. She carried a brown shopping bag and a long, aluminium crutch.

Trevor's fear of heights swamped his mind, clouding his vision. He lost his footing, dropping down a little with a violent thud. Herbert began to slide through Trevor's loosening grip. Reciting a prayer, Trevor pulled Herbert into him. He shoved his trainers into two new spaces in the Valdorama's steel frame.

'That was close, Herb!' he said, sucking in another long breath.

'What's going on down there?' Herbert asked, not wanting to look down.

'I think some old lady's going wild,' Trevor replied.

160

'Oh no, I think know her,' Herbert said, staring into Trevor. 'She's off her trolley! It's a long story but she caused all this. But at least we're safe up here.'

'I hope so, Herb,' Trevor replied.

TWENTY THREE

On the ground, Mrs Hunter hobbled up to the fire engine. She whirled her crutch around, knocking people out of the way. Two chatting fire fighters confronted her. But with a whooshing karate chop, she floored them both, knocking them down like skittles.

She scrambled onto the back of the fire engine, just as the long, aluminium ladder was swinging around on the top. At its end, a female fire fighter strapped her legs to its rungs.

Still clutching her crutch and bag, Mrs Hunter dragged her body onto the top of the engine. She grabbed hold of two big metal hooks, climbing up a small ladder. She stood on the top of the machine, snarling like a hungry wolf.

'Nobody messes with Hilary Hunter and gets away with it!' she yelled, waving her lethal crutch through the air.

Mrs Hunter screamed out a loud battle cry, goading the baying crowd. 'Yes, it may be unbelievable, viewers,' a TV reporter screamed into his microphone. 'But the scene you're watching is happening LIVE as I speak!'

Pulling her shoulders back, Mrs Hunter aimed her crutch at Herbert and Trevor. Launching her deadly weapon at her target, she grunted as it left her hand. The crutch missed its mark, plunging into the Valdorama before bouncing to the ground.

Mrs Hunter opened up her shopping bag. She pulled out a toffee apple by its stick. She flung it at Herbert and Trevor, like a strawberry hand grenade. She produced more ammunition, tossing the toffee apples up into the air.

Throwing her sticky bombs at her target, she danced with delight, whipping up the crowd. A hard toffee apple crashed into Herbert's leg. Then one ploughed into his stomach. Trevor twisted his body around, trying to shield Herbert from the bombardment.

A hard toffee apple hit Trevor's nose. His eyes started to water. He closed them up, coughing and spluttering. Sparks and stars danced around his head. His vision suddenly blurred. His big hands lost their strength, releasing their grip on the Valdorama's frame.

'Hang on Trevor!' Herbert screeched. 'We're falling!'

Shaking his head, Trevor managed to hang on. 'Don't you worry, Herb,' he gasped, gripping the cold steel. 'I won't let go of you.'

Mrs Hunter fished out her final two toffee apples, licking their glazed, toffee casings.

'Nobody steals my walking stick and gets away with it!' she screeched, taking aim. 'And my hat!'

Drawing her arms back, she tossed the two toffee apples towards Herbert and Trevor, this time scoring a bulls-eye.

One of the toffee apples battered Trevor's stomach, bouncing off his layers of fat. But the next sticky missile crashed into his face, knocking him clean out. Trevor released his grip on Herbert. Trevor's body plunged towards the earth like an out of control, spiralling aeroplane.

'Trevor!' Herbert screamed, spinning around. 'Noooo!'

With record-breaking speed, Trevor's fingers grabbed onto the Valdorama's steel arches. 'Trevor!' Herbert screamed again as tears spat out of his eyes.

Sobbing, Herbert struggled to hang on. His muscles ached and throbbed with sharp, pinprick pain. But his strength was fading. Fast.

TWENTY FOUR

The female fire fighter pulled a lever. The long ladder hissed into action, swinging around. Mrs Hunter was standing in the way, still balanced on the top of the engine. The fire fighter pushed the lever back up and the ladder clanked to an abrupt halt.

A chief fire fighter, wearing a white helmet, climbed onto the roof of his engine. He rugby tackled Mrs Hunter, wrapping his arms around her waist. Wailing, she collapsed into a heap on the fire engine's roof. The Fire chief lowered her body onto the ground, into the arms of the two police officers.

'Help!' Herbert cried, his fingers slipping. 'I can't hold on any longer.'

The enormous aluminium ladder swung around, cranking upwards. Herbert belched out a high-pitched yelp. His fingers released their grip. He plunged towards the ground. But in the nick of time, the female fire fighter grabbed hold of his legs. She pulled Herbert towards her, quickly strapping him to the end of the ladder.

As the ladder descended, Herbert noticed a group of Paramedics. They were crowding around Trevor, who was lying still on a stretcher, covered up with a red, fluffy blanket.

As soon as the ladder brushed the top of the fire engine, Herbert unstrapped himself. 'Hey, come back here!' the female fire fighter shouted as Herbert clambered down a small ladder.

'Trevor!' Herbert shouted, wiping away his tears with his sleeve.

Herbert dropped to the ground. He sprinted towards a small crowd gathered around Trevor. 'Let me through!' he demanded, barging into two fire fighters. But he couldn't go any further.

Swamped by a whole army of people, Herbert was trapped. Newspaper reporters jostled him, shoving their microphones into his face. A man balancing a TV camera on his shoulder barged into him, almost tripping him up.

'Stay back, please!' the police sergeant shouted out, catching hold of Herbert's hand. 'You can have your interviews later.'

The short, chunky officer led Herbert towards his lifesaver. 'Trevor!' Herbert cried, kneeling down in the balding, dusty grass. Massaging Trevor's big shoulders, Herbert's fingers pressed into him, attempting to wake him up.

'I think he's out cold,' a Paramedic announced, patting Herbert on the back. 'But I think your brave dad's just saved your life!'

'Err, yes, I know,' Herbert answered, not pulling his eyes away from Trevor's pale face.

'Photograph for the fairground's newsletter!' a tall man shouted out. Brandishing a large camera, he pointed its long lens at Herbert and Trevor. He seemed to appear from nowhere, his oversized, pin stripe suit hanging off his stick insect body.

'Smile please!' the photographer said. He snapped away several times, his bright flash punching into the fading light. Then he disappeared into the mass of people.

Trevor opened up his dark, glazed eyes, his eyelids flickering into life. 'I did it, Herb,' he mumbled. 'I saved you, mate.'

Then he closed his eyes, his big, stubbly head falling to one side.

TWENTY FIVE

'What's wrong with him?' Herbert yelled. 'Will he be all right?'

'It's a miracle,' a young Paramedic lady said, picking up the stretcher with her male colleague. 'I think it's a broken leg but he's had a *very* lucky escape.'

'It's as if he landed on a giant sponge or something,' her male colleague added.

'Well I'm not leaving him,' Herbert said, grabbing hold of Trevor's limp hand.

Mum burst through the crowd. She sprinted towards Herbert, her long legs galloping like a greyhound. Reaching him, she threw her long arms around his body.

She hugged into her son for an age, her body vibrating as she sobbed and sobbed. Tears, mixed with black mascara, rolled down her face, forming two stretching, black lines.

'I was watching it all on the news from my hospital bed,' she whimpered. 'When I suddenly realised who it was.'

'What happened to you, Mum?' Herbert asked, still holding his hero's hand. But his mum didn't answer. Her mind was filling up with a thousand thoughts.

She turned towards Trevor, still lying motionless on his stretcher. She stroked his fat, unshaven face. Then she planted a gentle kiss on his forehead, following the Paramedics towards the ambulance. 'Trevor saved my life, Mum,' Herbert said. 'They say he's got a broken leg and - '

As Herbert rattled on, his mum halted the Paramedics. Leaning over the stretcher, she stroked Trevor's chest, whispering into his ear, her voice soft and soothing.

'I've only just realised something,' she said, her black tears still streaming. 'I love you Trevor, I love you very much!'

171

Trevor stirred, his chest rising and falling. He grunted as a microscopic smile appeared on his face. Then his head rolled to one side as he returned to a deep, slumbering sleep.

Soon, Trevor was in the back of an ambulance, speeding to the local hospital. Sitting by his side, Herbert and his mum gazed at their unexpected superhero.

'Trevor saved my life, Mum,' Herbert said again, his body rattling up and down in the speeding ambulance. A thick film of tears covered his eyes, splashing onto his cheeks.

'I told you he was all right weeks ago, love,' Mum said, pinching her son's nose. 'He's just a great big softie really! But you wouldn't believe me, would you?'

'I know Mum; I'm really sorry,' Herbert said, putting his hands into his pockets. 'Oh, I've forgotten about this,' he said, pulling out Madame Mistral's small, golden envelope.

'What's that?' Mum asked.

172

'Madame Mistral handed it to me,' Herbert said. 'At the end when - '

'Oh not that old witch!' Mum snapped. 'Just look at all the trouble she's caused us! But what's in it? I'm intrigued.'

'What time is it?' Herbert asked.

'Twenty five past six,' his mum replied. 'Why?'

'Oh nothing,' Herbert replied, spreading his lips into a wry smile.

Herbert peeled open the envelope's flap and a little folded piece of parchment popped out of its home. Herbert unfolded it. Staring at it, his eyes grew wider.

On one side of the paper was a rough pencil sketch. It showed Herbert hanging from the Valdorama, with the words *Famous at last* underneath. Trevor's figure was falling towards the ground. Herbert's dad was underneath him, hovering like an angel, his arms outstretched. *Just be yourself* was scrawled underneath it.

On the other side of the paper was a letter, handwritten in a neat, cursive style script:

To my beloved
Suzanne and Herbert,

I love you and I'm always watching you. Never forget that! Trevor's a great guy. He's got a good, genuine heart, so look after him - you all deserve each other! Great times are just around the corner. Believe it and it will happen!

PS

I loved meeting you today, Herbert. I'm so proud of you. You don't half make me smile! Just look at the photograph in front of you. That's proof that I'm always around, even though you can't see me!

Lots of love, Daddy xxx

Herbert glanced around. There it was, in front of him. The photograph for the fairground's newsletter, stuck to the wall of the ambulance. Narrowing his eyes, Herbert peered into its glossy surface.

There was Herbert, kneeling down, at the side of Trevor's stretcher. Herbert's dad was standing behind. His arms were wrapped around Herbert and Trevor, bathed in a warm, golden sunlight. A huge, proud smile arched his lips and a silver, misty haze surrounded his body.

A ghostly silence fell from the heavens, resting upon Herbert, his mum and Trevor. Herbert and his mum stared into each other's damp eyes. As they embraced, their tears mixed, forming a pure and powerful potion of love.

'I think that's the sign you were looking for, Herb,' his mum sniffed, squeezing her son's hands. 'Your dad likes Trevor too, so that's great!'

Herbert looked up at the ambulance's clean, white ceiling. 'I love you, Dad,' he whispered, raising his eyebrows. He grabbed hold of Trevor's limp hand, rubbing it with his thumb. 'And thanks for sending us Trevor,' he said, staring at his hero's face. 'He's a great guy; I know that now.'

A loud, piercing siren burst into life as the ambulance approached a busy set of traffic lights. Herbert's and his mum's eyes peered into each other once more, their lips spreading into warm, infectious smiles.

They both cast their gaze over their unexpected hero, his stomach slowly rising and falling. Their journey to the hospital was almost over.

But their journey together was
only just beginning...

EPILOGUE

Whatever happened to old Mrs Hunter and our dear old friend, the mysterious, magical, and perhaps marvellous Madame Mistral?

Mrs Hunter was arrested. She now spends her days in a comfortable old people's home. She has a new walking stick that's chained to her wrist. However, she's still searching for her favourite green hat. Police believe her hat may be in a nest on a cliff-top somewhere.

Detectives know the name of the thief too – a brown spotted seagull, who goes by the name of 'Cyril'.

He's also wanted for a series of crimes, often taking place at seaside towns and resorts. This year alone, he's stolen 357 ice creams, 243 donuts and 128 pork pies out of people's fingers. And he's also dropped white, sloppy bombs onto 872 tourists!

The magical and mysterious Madame Mistral has never been heard of since. Nobody at the fairground had even heard of her. Her little tent seemed to vanish into thin air. But she's out there somewhere.

So if you ever bump into a fortune-teller at a travelling fairground, beware. Ask yourself these important questions:

Is she wearing a tight, yellow headband, with a collection of rubies on the front?

Does she enjoy drinking cups of tea?

Does she possess an old dinosaur bone, which once belonged to Arkhad?

If the answer is 'yes', then please, have nothing whatsoever to do with her. Especially if she asks you this seemingly innocent question:

What is your favourite animal?

Then again,

she might have a

Secret message,

just for you...

Lightning Source UK Ltd.
Milton Keynes UK
UKHW04f1146300718
326492UK00001B/228/P